Mere Kaffir

Apartheid: It's Not So Black and White

Keith Brown

To Fred
Best wishes

Keith

First published in Great Britain in 2013
by Shakspeare Editorial

ISBN: 978-1-291-67275-6 (paperback)

Cover design: Paul Godney / @paulgodney

This title is also available as an ebook.

Fundraising for orphans

Thank you for purchasing this copy of *Mere Kaffir*. 100% of the profits from the sale of this book will be used to assist Aids orphans and their carers at the non-profit Siyabakhulisa Care Centre in Mimosadale, Estcourt, Natal in South Africa. We provide food, clothing and welfare to, on average, 90 to 120 orphans in the area. Thank you for helping us with our fight against poverty and deprivation.

Further information may be found on the charities page at **www.keithbrownspeaking.com**

Preface

Having worked, lived and suffered under South African apartheid I discovered a great deal, not only about myself and the flaws within my own humanity but also just how deep rooted and ingrained our judgements and attitudes about other people and cultures really are.

Far from being a simple black and white issue, the apartheid years actually gave the world a benchmark with regard to a declared level of racist attitude. Yet, how can it be a black and white issue when I, as a white European, was labelled by many of my then peers as a 'white kaffir'?

The word kaffir, sometimes spelt kaffer or kafir, is derived from the Arabic term kafir, which means 'disbeliever', or literally 'one who conceals the truth that all human beings are born equal and their lives have equal value'. Once it was a neutral term for black Southern African people, but is now considered a racial or ethnic slur and is most commonly used as an offensive term for a black person in South Africa and other African countries.

I decided to write this book as a novel to describe a level of inhumanity and hatred that sometimes beggars belief. None of the characters are actual representations of real individuals, they have grown out of my reflections on real situations. It has taken over two years to write the book but decades to decipher my own understanding of what I truly learnt from the early days of my life.

My hope is that this book will help others to take a deeper look within themselves and consider their own true reason and purpose for life. We all have our dreams and goals; as a young man mine was to seek fame and fortune in the gold mines of Southern Africa, but the true value of what I found there was not measured in dollars per ounce but in the depth of humanity; in the unexpected love and mutual respect that was created when people, irrespective of personal belief, colour and culture, are drawn together through intimidation and intolerance in order to survive.

Our human lives are but a shadow and a wisp of smoke in comparison to the age of the earth and the treasures lying buried under millions of years of evolutionary change. Each generation in its time demands its right to life, riches and fame, to own and hoard wealth or lands and sees itself as master of all things, even over the lives of others. Yet, so often in history, that has proven to be its undoing.

When man first struck a blow at the Earth's crust and discovered the variety of metals it contained there came with it the desire to have more and be more. Their value was initially attached to what the metals could do to simplify and assist in the personal lives of those mining them, like bronze axes, but it would not be long before that value altered. They then provided the few with an opportunity to exploit the many on a monumental scale, mainly for the benefit of that few. The sparkle and wonderment of the world and its most precious resource, gold, would darken men's hearts and souls with so much greed, that men's lives would become valued in grams per ton.

It is in this setting that our story begins, in the early 1980s in a country still entrenched in an apartheid era begun in 1948. It would be another decade before the end of an evil regime that cost the lives and souls of many people in a, seemingly on the surface, black and white divide. A regime like many others in mankind's history that had its roots in man's most common and destructive enemy of all, simple fear.

The similarities between the meerkat, which are only found in Southern Africa, and the political regime and the gold mining industry of the time are quite striking. Meerkats work and live underground, they are very territorial and extremely tribal in their behaviour and vicious to other meerkat tribes. They are fiercely protective and take good care of their own.

Is that not a similar situation to that evidenced during the 1970 race riots in the UK? The reality is that tribalism is still alive and well in our world and the use of South Africa in that infamous period for this story is only by way of example.

Do our own personal desires and need for more of the world's treasures perhaps blind us to a self-evident truth? That we are but temporary custodians, no matter what we own or what riches we have gained. As we walk through this life we will fight many battles of our own, like the book's central character, Matt Davis, in his search for true reason and purpose as he tries to understand and discover what is truly valuable in life.

At the end of this battle for life, will there be any evidence to convict us personally of being a Mere Kaffir?

Terms and allusions

2000 psi .... pressure at 2000 pounds per square inch

Baas .... boss/leader

Banksman........................ controls the loading of men and materials onto the lift

Basotho .... native tribe

Biltong............................. dried beef strips, a local delicacy

Boer................................. Afrikaner of Dutch descent

Braai .... barbeque

Carbon leader.................. type of ore body

Change house .... locker rooms

Conglomerate .... type of rock formation

Drives and cross cuts .... types of tunnels, running to north, south, east and west of the shaft

Fanagalo.......................... a pidgin language used in South Africa mines, for simpler communication between the tribes

Fault plane....................... a natural break in a rock layer that moves the gold up or down

Footwall .... floor of the tunnel

Gold bar .... valuable gold ore

Gold bearing ore.............. rock containing gold elements

Gold grade....................... value of gold ore in grams per ton

Hanging wall .... roof of the tunnel

Iron pyrite .... fool's gold

Kaffirs .... derogatory name for native people

Kaffir booty .... lover of kaffirs

Kraal .... Zulu village

Machine operators........... drilling machine operators

Mine cage .... lift to travel underground

Mine captain .... supervisor over the mine reporting to the mine manager

Mine car .... used for transporting broken ore

Mine shaft........................ excavation from the surface down to the ore body

Misfire.............................. the face does not blast

Nunakula .... God, the creator of all things, in Fanagalo

Official's club .... recreational club for shift bosses and mine captains

Ore passes .... a rock holding bin

Outcropped .... when the ore body has been exposed at the surface level

Pikanin .... assistant in Zulu, means a small child

Plasse Boer .... farm Boer, derogatory remark

Pommies........................... British subjects

Rand................................. South African currency

Reef .... another name for gold ore or ore body

Rooi necks......................... rednecks, also British subjects

Sacky Sacky...................... Afrikaner traditional music and dancing

Sangoma .... witch doctor

Seismic event .... earthquake or ground movement

Shabean .... illegal bar and brothel

Shift boss......................... supervisor over a number of white contractors and black operators, reporting to the mine captain

Shona .... native tribe

Sidewall .... sides of the tunnel

Sjamboks .... clubs used for giving beatings

Slow burners..................... burn for about four hours, look like an oversized tampon about a foot long with a small hole at one end to put the ignitor cord through

Station .... a station is a point of exit from the shaft to the various working places known as levels (a shaft can have up to 10 or 15 stations throughout its depth)

Stope face .... a gold face where ore is drilled and blasted

Vetkoeks........................... fat cake or doughnut

Winze .... a small tunnel driven into the floor at the same angle as the ore body

Xhosa, Zulu .... different native tribes

Chapter 1

The sound of the wheels of the 747 landing at Jan Smuts, Johannesburg jolted Matt Davis out of his slumber after an overlong flight of some twelve hours. It was the time of apartheid and black-governed countries on the African continent forbade the use of their airspace to South African-bound planes in answer to the call to end a crumbling apartheid regime. One in which he personally had only one real interest, to claim his fame and fortune, but that would have a greater effect on him than he would ever dare to imagine.

His life had been materially sparse as a young white boy in the 1960s mining town of Beaverbrook on the Yorkshire/Nottinghamshire border in England and had left him with an embittered spirit as the only child needing free school meals. Something that was seized upon by the other children in cruel indifference and even by the teaching staff, who made Matt stand in his own queue behind those who needed no such handouts and saw nothing wrong in the flagrant intimidation of the poor. This intimidation suffered in his younger years was to prove minor compared to the emotional trauma he would soon endure under South African apartheid.

Does fortune favour the brave or is it the fortunate few who exploit the brave? Academically that would have been a question beyond Matt, a simple man with a simple aim, work and get money. A strong work ethic was natural to him. Yes, he was greedy for more out of life, but is greed really greed when you are truly prepared to do whatever it takes to better your lot in life? Are there no boundaries to the way we pursue our goal to achieve more wealth?

The underachieving Matt had been challenged, both materially and emotionally, by his friends (friends who had been sleeping secretly with his wife) as to the dangers he might face in his exploits extracting the world's most precious commodity. He had remarked, 'Dangers, what dangers? I spit in the eye of danger.' How quickly he would learn that danger tends to spit back. Matt, however, had a great inner strength and tenacity and a feeling that he could be so much more and do so much more if he only had the chance to prove it. The future would prove that he was, in fact, more intelligent than his reach-for-the-sky eldest brother, Stephen, who seldom appeared to fail at anything. Matt had yet to truly believe that of himself, or understand that there were forces working on his behalf that he could never have imagined.

Matt was born the middle one of three to Mary and Mike Davis in March 1963. His father beat a hasty exit into another marriage when he was three, which meant that Matt would grow up without a true father figure since his elder brother, being only one year older, would not be taking up any kind of mantle as the leader of the home. The absence of a true father figure had left Matt with a deep sense of loneliness. He was a bit of lad who could hold his own in a fist fight if he had no choice, but there was never an 'I will get my dad onto you' like the other kids would say, Matt was on his own with that one.

However, Matt did know the occasional brutality of a mother's lover, which created a deep hatred in his heart and a yet deeper desire to prove that he was not a 'good for nothing, waste of space, loser' as blows rained down from those that his mother had relationships with over the years, but who didn't want to step up to the mark and be real father figures. This systematic violence was par for the course throughout his teenage years as Matt was the one who could seldom keep his mouth shut, his brain often being in neutral at the time. Not that his other siblings missed out on the beatings but they had the good sense to get out of the house at every opportunity. This dysfunctional background gave birth to a scenario, familiar to less academic siblings, of job prospects limited to the coal mine or, if you were fortunate and well enough connected, the railways. Matt had no such connections so the colliery was his only option.

Marriage at nineteen to his first and only girlfriend added insult to injury. She was the first girl he'd had sex with – after three pints at the miner's welfare social club in the glorious surroundings of her auntie's coal shed. He'd never been much of a drinker. On hearing the glad news his co-workers at Sinfield Colliery – where he had started work aged sixteen – quipped, 'Sarah Roberts? She spent so much time in that coal shed her auntie bought her a pair of knee pads for Christmas! We all thought you were a twat, but now we know it.'

His self-esteem was at an all-time low as his elder brother Stephen – a naturally bright man who did not have to try too hard – was busy scaling the dizzy heights as a Sergeant in the Royal Marines. Still, Matt determined to make something of his life. 'Just wait and see,' he told his piss-taking colleagues.

His five foot six inch frame was wiry but strong as he stood in St John's the Martyr Church on his wedding day, 26th March 1982, but his heart and spirit were embittered. What was he doing there? He bit down on his lower lip. Six days prior to the wedding the pending offspring had been stillborn, making an already obviously pointless marriage even more so. If there is a God up there, he pondered, he knows I'm lying, but he had not the gumption to back out now. His new wife's family had reluctantly fronted the cost of the buffet and her three elder brothers had already read him the route plan to pain and suffering should he even pass wind in the wrong direction as regards their bloodline. He felt completely lost and hopeless, everything inside him was crying out why, why are you doing this? The answer was simple, he was a coward and he knew it.

His appearance did not reflect his personality, what you saw was not what you got. He had been brought up on violence and derision, which had created a violent and explosive temperament his stature could not back up. That had often resulted in him taking a real beating, from Sarah's elder brother on one occasion. Yet in those battles he would be trying to rain blows on the very things in his opponent that he hated about himself, shadowboxing his own failures and shortcomings. On the surface he appeared arrogant, self-obsessed and emotionally lacking. However, they were only self-preservation mechanisms to help him endure the circumstances into which he was born and that hid the deep desperation of a man who loved deeply and was emotionally sensitive. Within himself Matt believed he had a destiny. That he was born to be and do more than many would give him credit for. What he showed the world was not what was in his heart, Matt's soul cried out for the very basic of human needs: love and acceptance. He often asked himself, 'why am I not accepted and loved for who I am?' How true it is that many who cannot even spell those words, often through little fault of their own, need to experience them more than those who can.

Matt's underachievement was obvious in comparison with his siblings and his schoolmates. His schooling had been erratic at best as he struggled with basic English and maths. This had created a deep resentment about the lack of material wealth in his life compared to other family members. His desire for material goods was almost idolatrous in that he was determined to prove his worth in life with the houses, cars and money that he would earn through his new venture in the gold mines of South Africa. Would Matt Davis find his reason and purpose there, making a new life with his white South African brothers?

His mother's last words to him some eighteen months before, her body ravaged by cancer, were that she believed in him. She had told him that respect can be earned by hard work, although sadly during her life material gains didn't follow. Those born to the grind are seldom able to climb out. She died regretting that things could have been different for her and the son she loved the most and fearing that her own failings would play out again in his life. He assured her that his name would be in lights one day. She responded with her last laboured breath, 'Find the truth my son and the truth will set you free.'

'What truth?' he asked through the mammoth tears and heartbreak of a man losing the woman he loved most in the world, now and forever. But her spirit had left and she was already in the hands of God.

As the plane taxied Matt was still waking and he heard the sound of the finest silk being crumpled in rough and calloused hands. The sound was there and gone within moments but resounded in his ears and penetrated deep within. His eyes, now wide open, sought for the source as the cabin crew requested all to stay in their seats until the plane had come to a complete standstill. Matt breathed in deeply and slumped back into his seat looking over to his reluctant travelling companion and spouse Sarah, who had other ideas about the many offerings of Africa as she eyed-up the blonde, blue-eyed member of the cabin crew, Mark. The one she'd had running around all night with her constant requests for the complimentary wine and food.

'My arse is like a plank, how did you sleep?' he asked.

'Like you care, unlike Mark,' who was in earshot, 'he knows how to take care of a girl.'

Yes, Sarah was sure that there was something in this little venture that she could treat as an extended holiday. This failure of a husband of hers would need to work all hours to keep her in a lifestyle she believed she was entitled to. She was confident she would be adorned with the finest gold in no time.

The air was crisp and warm, not humid as Matt had expected. It was winter and the average day time temperature was around eighteen degrees. The earth surrounding the grassed area, which looked terribly dry, was dark red in contrast to the black and brown soil of the counties where he had roamed as a child.

'This is it, all things are new, even the soil is different,' he thought, turning to see where Sarah was. She stood exchanging a final wink and flirtatious comments with Mark as she left the aircraft. 'Well, most things are new,' he thought. 'Do they have coal houses in Africa?

Mrs Van dar Westheizen met them at the airport with transport back to the mine offices at West Rand Consolidated Mines just outside Potchefstroom, about two hours from Johannesburg. She was a woman of presence – resembling a headmistress who had tanned his backside a few times at Mountfield Junior School – but she was warm in a strange way and the smile seemed genuine enough.

Sarah's face went thunderous as Mrs Van dar Westheizen – who had allowed them to call her Lynette – explained that they were now leaving the bright lights and debauchery of the capital city for the cleaner and the more God-fearing countryside. This was where the mine and all those who work on it lived, except the blacks who live in compounds. Matt wondered if they were similar to barracks for soldiers.

'You will have no trouble with them. They are just labourers, carriers of stones and hewers of wood, described in Joshua, in the Bible, as "servants and they have no crown in their hair", did you know that? We call them kaffirs because they are less than God's creatures, although our pastor does not like that word to be used in church on Sunday. He will use it openly during the rest of week however, as we all do. Are you believers in the love of God?' she asked.

Chapter 2

The mine house they were assigned was substantial in European terms with four bedrooms and a bathroom. The decor was a little old fashioned and the fittings definitely bore no resemblance to modern design, but it was clean and sturdy. The garden was quite extensive and well-cultivated with mature flowerbeds and shrubs.

'And where is the pool? You said everyone has a pool in South Africa,' Sarah complained to Matt.

'Swimming pools are only for senior managers,' remarked Lynette. 'Your husband is an immigrant mine worker, which is the lowest tier of white worker on the mine. But there is one good thing, when you start at the bottom there is only one way and that is up.' But there was no conviction as to that possibility in her voice. 'My husband and son both work on the mine. My Victor is the mining engineer and my son Joshua, like in the Bible, is a junior electrical engineer. You probably won't be bumping into them anytime soon as they are considered officials and have different office accommodation and changing facilities at the mine than the general white miners. Your furniture will arrive in the next two to four days, depending on how quickly I can get the paperwork done. In the meantime, you are welcome to stay at the hotel in town at the mine's expense. It is only a three star but it is clean,' she said, exiting the door.

Sarah stood, mouth open, a rare occasion her being stuck for words.

'Not what I initially expected,' said Matt, 'but it will get better.'

'On the basis that it cannot get worse,' retorted Sarah. 'Four days in that shithole of a hotel we passed on the way in. I hope they have twin beds because you are not sleeping in mine.'

'I almost forgot,' Lynette said, popping her head back through the door. 'The Mine Captain is expecting you at the mine tomorrow morning at five thirty. His name is Nigel Lloyd Symington, but as an immigrant mine worker you must refer to him as Meneer, that means Sir in Afrikaans, and if you want some good advice don't be late.'

***

Matt was woken from his slumber at the hotel by that sound of crushing silk he had heard on his arrival only the day before. 'A new day, a new opportunity and into the hand of God,' he remarked, not knowing why. His sleeping wife responded by turning over.

'Morning Meneer,' said Matt, entering Symington's office for the first time at number six shaft, remembering Mrs Van dar Westheizen's warning about how he must greet his new superior. The walls were covered with mining plans that made little sense to Matt, as he scanned them asking, 'What is that area to the west of the shaft marked in red, does that mean danger?' he asked nervously.

Looking not unlike a bloated weasel, Symington was small, balding and overweight, evidence of a fondness for red meat, five star brandy and vetkoeks, a local doughnut type treat or fat cake. Coupled with his aversion to any kind of manual work he was a heart attack in the making. 'That, you pommie bastard runt, is no concern of yours. Don't think for one minute that the fact that you have a white skin means I think you are any more than just a white kaffir. You have been given to me by head office against my better judgement. The British always bring a boat load of hypocritical "all men are born equal" bullshit when you come to Africa. You lot simply having forgotten the blood and violence the Empire meted out in pursuit of an ideal for their so-called sovereign that was not any different to Hitler's.' He thought briefly then continued, 'It was you pompous and pious bastards that set up the first concentration camps for the prisoners taken in the Boer War, where some of these men's forefathers and families died.' He pointed to some obvious Afrikaners in the room, dressed in safari shorts, knee high socks and brown leather dirt boots. 'Just remember, the blacks probably hate you just a fraction less than I do and will slit your throat for a sixpence.'

Matt stood speechless, incapable of processing that outburst as all but one of the bystanders nodded in full agreement.

'I will give only one piece of advice. Remember this, that no man can kill a man like a black man. Koos,' he looked at his shift boss, 'take this pommie out of my sight and sort him out a place to work.'

The room fell silent.

'But no one wants to work with a salt peel!' exclaimed Venter. 'Not any whites at least.'

'You see what I mean?' Symington gazed with disdain at Matt. 'That is how we see you here. You salty cocks have one foot in England and one foot in South Africa and your dicks hang in the ocean in-between.'

Symington had seemingly forgotten that he was a 'when we', the nickname white South Africans gave to all ex-Rhodesians with their 'when we were in Rhodesia' stories, constantly reminding them of their perfect republic that the world never officially recognised. A man of vile, alcohol-fuelled tempers that his five foot two frame could not physically back up. His power as a mine overseer was his only armour, along with the mandate for severe beatings to all who stepped out of line. The beatings would be meted out by his whipping boys, the shift bosses (especially Venter), who never failed to achieve their bonus payments each month. If the blacks got really out of line it would be his Basotho Boys' Brigade who would be tasked with getting things back in line.

'I will take him,' said the reluctant voice of Dirk Grayling, the other shift boss in the room. He had stood gazing at the floor the whole time, only lifting his eyes when Symington seemed to imply he was one of the locals.

'You had better come with me,' the large and overweight Grayling looked Matt in the eye as he walked past him towards to door. The deflated Matt followed, as a lamb is silent before its shearer.

'I want it!' screamed Symington, smashing his silver-knobbed black cane onto the mine planning table. The force placed a small dent in both table and knob, tearing the plan in the red-marked area mirrored in the plan on the wall. Matt half-turned before being pulled back by Grayling.

'Ask no questions and keep out of that. You're not wanted or welcome here so keep your mouth shut and do as you are told. I will give you six months before you go crawling back to that . . . Where do you come from again?'

'Nottingham,' said Matt, now completely subdued; ten thousand miles to be told no one wanted you, he thought.

'Oh yes, Nottingham. Did anything good ever come out of there?'

'Well, Robin Hood I suppose.'

'He was just a fairy tale and that, my pommie friend, is where the fairy tale ends for you, because this is Africa. I hope you have got balls the size of a lion because there are no merry men here,' Grayling concluded.

Matt asked Grayling what had put Symington into such a temper and was surprised by the taciturn man's fulsome reply.

'He is the son of an ex-Rhodesian politician, mine owner and one of Africa's richest men, Cecil Lloyd Symington who died before Rhodesian independence. His father had been a corrupt man of few morals who had managed to pay off government and high-ranking legal officials, escaping accusations of embezzlement of mining and water rights belonging to the Shona. Nigel and his mother fled to South Africa penniless as the new Zimbabwe government officials seized their assets. He cannot stand blacks of whatever tribe, or pommies as turncoats about Rhodesia.'

The men walked for several metres, looking at the red earth, before Grayling broke the silence by saying, 'First, two weeks in the mine school learning that kaffir's language, Fanagalo, and then I will put you on the contract on twelve, level six, west drive and cross cut tunnels. Joseph is the team leader there, he is as good as a kaffir gets but most of the management don't really trust him. No one really knows where he came from, the rumours are that he is the son of a chief who died in police custody and that he had a son who died in Leibritz mine, where Venter was at the time. Joseph just turned up one day, a godsend really as we had real problems with the kaffirs at the time, but they respect him and do what he says. We pay him more than the rest and rumour has it he shares it with his own Zulu team leaders, but that is his affair as long as he toes the line and the job gets done. The mine school is over there,' he pointed to a range of brick buildings with red tin roofs. 'Ask for Ben Jordan, he runs it. Come back to me in two weeks.'

And off Grayling went, into the official's change house where their lockers were.

Chapter 3

Two weeks later

'Malo Joseph, kanjani?' Matt said morning to Joseph and asked how his team leader was. Two weeks in mine school had furnished him with a blasting certificate and a limited understanding of the mine language. Joseph replied courteously and then talked for two minutes in Fanagalo. Matt understood not a bloody word and just swallowed hard when it seemed it was time to respond. He rummaged in his pocket for his English to Fanagalo phrase book and flipped through its pages but they shed no light. Joseph simply nodded his head that Matt should follow him but Matt was stopped in his tracks by a wiry, red-faced banksman whose job it was to control the travel of men and material down the shaft.

'Where you going?' he asked.

'On the cage,' replied Matt.

'White men don't ride with kaffirs. You will catch the next one.'

Joseph's wry smile disappeared as the cage descended only feet from where Matt was standing.

'Here comes the Nazi,' remarked the banksman just under his breath.

Matt turned for his first sighting of the formidable figure of the mousey-haired mine manager, Jan Coetzee, whose square-jawed, six foot ten, eighteen stone Afrikaner frame ran the whole show. Matt had been warned about him by a friendly South African fellow learner in the mine school, who had described Coetzee as a complete bastard with an unhealthy, tense relationship with Symington. Although Symington had more influence with the board of directors – since Symington's father had had them all on the payroll at one time or another – it was actually Coetzee who held what Symington really wanted, his father's mining rights, lost to Coetzee in a drunken card game some twenty years before.

The banksman's initial bravery quickly gave way to fidgeting and nervousness the closer Coetzee got. His big frame ate up the ground with a pace that made it appear like he was running. 'Move,' he said, pushing Matt out of the way as he went to the tally sheets to see how many skips of ore had been hoisted on the night shift.

'It was a good night,' said the dessicated banksman whose nickname, Biltong, was scrawled at the bottom of the tally sheets and in various places around his cabin. 'Forty skips and we are still pulling.'

Coetzee didn't take his eyes off the tally sheet, 'Forty skips of shit. And the grade of the ore is about four grams per ton. We need six at least to break even.' He barked, 'Where is that geologist Berriman, the pommie bastard?'

'He is already underground, Meneer,' said Biltong, 'he said he was going to six east, six face to do some sampling.'

'Get out the way.' Coetzee pushed back in Matt's direction, even though there were exits in all directions and made his way at a pace back to the mine offices.

The bravery returned to Biltong as he said, 'Nazi pig. He thinks no one knows about all his antics with young black kaffir girls. He says he hates blacks but most of the half-caste lepers you see around the town are down to that German half-breed pig.'

Biltong began to tell Matt about how Coetzee's father had been a mine manager but left his family penniless as he entered an alcoholic's early grave; and how that had meant that he'd got kicked out of boarding school at Potchefstroom and been brought up by his mother's partner after she died suddenly. A vicious man apparently who would beat and sodomise him regularly.

'It is no wonder he is a lunatic, we are all what we believe ourselves to be,' said Biltong, 'and that man believes he is a white god of a superior race. But the reality is that he is an evil man and I pity his wife and children. He might go to church on Sunday and sing all the songs but he has only one god and that is money. He wants his gold out and he doesn't care that much how many bodies come out with it. We had forty fatals last year, not that he would be shedding any tears. He'd never have stopped production except for the fact that a white miner named Seibritz was trapped and bleeding to death under a huge roof fall and the mines inspector would be asking awkward questions as to the time of death. Seibritz lived long enough to be told by his rescuers that Venter was the real father of his two children.' After several seconds of silence he continued, 'That Venter is another one. He is like a cancer around this area, in his presence people die either physically or emotionally. There is real evil here you will see.'

'How do you know all this?' asked Matt, unconvinced by Biltong's ramblings.

'You calling me a liar?'

'No, you just you seem to know a lot about people's private lives.'

'Word carries quickly around here. There are few walls in the bush lands and gossip, lies and intimidation are the way most things get done around here. Like I said, you will see. And I have heard that Venter has already got your good lady wife in his sights, and she will fall under his charm, they all do,' he said as he pushed Matt into the cage and dropped the chain gate door in front of him.

Three quick rings and the cage descended, with Matt standing there speechless. Before the cage finally came to rest at six level Matt had concluded that he would have to truly watch his back here; no one was friendly and all seemed to have their own personal agendas. Symington's words came back to him, 'No man can kill a man like a black man'. What kind of statement was that? The worst kind Matt concluded, should it be true.

The day could not finish soon enough and Matt drove home quickly at the end of his shift. He met Venter's white Toyota pickup going in the opposite direction, his paddle-sized hands engulfing most of the steering wheel. He waved at Matt and gave the wryest of smiles.

'What did he want?' Matt demanded of Sarah.

'Who? Koos?' she answered.

'Koos? His name his Venter.'

'Well, if you were friendlier like me you would know his first name is Koos and at least he can be bothered to help me get the groceries into the house. I thought you said we were going to have a maid to do all the housework, like everybody else.'

'Forget that,' interrupted Matt, now even more irritated. 'What did he want?'

'Nothing. He just popped by to see if we had settled in okay and to ask if he could do anything to help as he is your shift boss.'

'He is not my shift boss Dirk Grayling is,' Matt said crossly, 'and I have heard bad things about him, never let him in here again.'

'You bring me all this way to Africa where I have no friends and the first person that is friendly to me you want to me to ignore,' retorted Sarah.

'Yes I do. Remember back home when my so-called best mate, Mick Lions, was kind enough to walk you home after that dance at the welfare when you'd had a bit too much to drink? You know which weekend, the one I had gone fishing, and all the rumours that were spread about him being found asleep in your Granny's coal house the following morning?'

'All horrid rumours. And you always bring that up!' shouted Sarah. 'You cannot be responsible for things that happen when you're drunk, everybody knows that.' She walked off into the bathroom.

'Well we don't need any kind of rumours and things around here. We have a plan to make our fortune and then get out of here, just like we discussed in England,' he shouted after her. His temper mellowed as he thought how the job was definitely not what he thought it was going to be, how dangerous it was in many ways and how no one really wanted him here. 'Do you know what I realised today, Sarah? Apartheid is not only about black and white skin. These Afrikaners hate everyone who is not Afrikaans, many of them speak about church and God and religion but they hate just about everyone. I saw that mine manager today, Coetzee. He is a scary man and no one seems to like him either, and do you know the rumours that are going around about him?'

Sarah stood, watching Matt's demeanour change to that of someone who seemed afraid. She saw her opportunity to win a point, something she had a reputation for doing one way or another. 'There you go, rumours! You will believe anything you will. He just might have got drunk as well, and it's probably not his fault either.'

'You are not really hearing this are you?'

'I am not interested. You brought us here, this is your dream not mine, so I bought myself these to cheer myself up.' She displayed an armful of new garments she had purchased at Edwards Stores.

'How much?'

Sarah quickly counted up the price tags, hugged the silk shirts to her chest and retorted softly, 'Six hundred rand.'

'That's half my salary as a learner miner,' he shouted.

'Well! I have nothing to wear until my clothes and everything come from England and I need something nice to wear at the braai on Saturday night.'

'What's a braai and what are you talking about?'

'Koos invited me to a braai, which is what they call a barbeque, at the official's club on Saturday night and I can take a guest or come alone he said.'

'You really are dim aren't you? Are you really telling me that you don't know what his intentions are?' Matt raised his eyebrows.

'I told you. He just wants to be friends.'

'Oh really? Do you think that the fact that you have great tits and an arse that most men would want to eat their dinner off would have anything to do with his reasons for friendship?' Matt replied sarcastically

'Just because that is all that you see when you look at me does not mean that others do the same, others see more to me than that.'

Although the idea that the very attractive and manly Koos would think that was already making Sarah fantasise a little. Her thoughts encouraged her to take Matt to the bedroom where she played out those fantasies while telling Matt of her unending love. Sarah liked her sex, and lots of it, and had worked out that a man performs so much better with plenty of encouragement. Especially telling him he was the best she had ever had, whether that was actually true or false. As a weak emotional man, often subservient to the directives of his spouse, Matt conformed to the well-known truth that when your tool is hard your brain is soft. The Saturday night braai was fixed in the diary. What harm could it really do?

Chapter 4

One month later

'Baas, baas!' shouted Joseph the following morning as half the black shift stood on the surface waiting to go down,

'What's going on Joseph? What are all these men doing here? They should have been underground an hour ago.'

'Mukulu nyaganyaga kona lapa panze,' Joseph replied.

As Matt tried to work out from his phrase book what that meant, the squeal from the tyres of four Land Rovers came across the yard. Six white security guys and two black assistants got out of the vehicles, accompanied by two of the biggest Rottweilers Matt had ever seen, with heads the size of young lions. They immediately started to bark and pull against the leashes that restrained them whenever a black man caught their attention. Matt asked a white officer what the problem was. The response in Afrikaans meant nothing to him. Whenever he asked a question in English when they did actually respond the answer would come back in Afrikaans and often others round about laughed out loud and Matt knew that they were taking the piss out of him. The security officer spoke again in Afrikaans as they took shotguns and semi-automatic weapons out of the back of the vehicles and proceeded towards the shaft and into the cage. They disappeared with three short rings of the signal bell. By that time Matt had worked out that Joseph had said, 'big trouble underground'.

Thirty minutes passed before the cage resurfaced and the chain gate lifted, the body of a dead Rottweiler was carried out by its white handler. The dog's fur was wet with blood from a wound to its throat and it glistened in the bright sunshine. The handler's eyes filled with tears as he lamented over his pride and joy. 'Bastard kaffirs,' he said several times before he disappeared into the back of a Land Rover. The other white security men emerged from the cage their gunbarrels still smoking and said to Biltong, 'We have left two down there to organise the bodies for retrieval.'

'Forget that! Those bastards have cost me enough time already, get the rest of this shift underground!' ordered Jan Coetzee in a venomous tone. He had made his way across the yard unnoticed, a rare occasion as his size eighteen wellington boots often announced his arrival long before his big frame was seen.

'There are seven dead, Meneer. Bloody tribes squabbling again. Sorry about that, but they would not come quietly,' said the head of the security team with a slight smirk on his face.

'Whatever,' replied Coetzee. 'Did the rest go into the work places?'

'Yes Meneer. We dispersed the rest with Rhino whips and smoke canisters. It is all quiet again now.'

'Biltong,' screamed Coetzee. 'Get these idle bastards underground. What are you waiting for? Davis,' he turned towards Matt, 'you work on level twelve do you not?'

'Er . . . yes, Meneer,' Matt was surprised, it was the first time Coetzee had actually spoken to him.

'Go with Biltong, get your pikanin and make sure the station is washed down and the bodies are out before I get down there in an hour.'

Before Matt could respond Coetzee was already engaged in another conversation with the mine captain who had just shown up. Symington's face looked flushed and greasy with sweat, brandy from the evening before was obviously still giving him a kicking.

'That stuff will kill you. Remember what happened to my father, if I was not the man I am he would have ruined my life too. The gold grade is shit and you're looking for the solution in a bottle of five star Martell. Shut up I'm talking!' Coetzee said as Symington tried to interject.

'No, I was just saying,' Symington ignored the order. 'I think we may have a solution for the grade problem but let us discuss that in your office.'

'It had better not be that fool's errand of looking for the Black Reef,' retorted Coetzee, 'you know my thoughts on that. It doesn't exist and we have enough trouble with these kaffirs without stirring up trouble with their myths and sangomas.'

'No, I hear what you saying but Berriman has found . . .'

'Berriman? Where is that pommie bastard geologist? He is hiding from me. All these poor grade are his fault. Six east six my arse, we have had nothing but trouble with that face and it is my reputation that is at stake.'

Their voices were lost to the bystanders as they walked across the yard to the mine offices. Matt and Biltong watched them disappear.

'Come on,' Biltong motioned to Matt. 'We had best get down there quick and get it sorted out.'

Matt reluctantly got into the cage. Having to deal with seven dead bodies was not what he had envisaged as part of his job as he had sat on the A52 coal face just three months ago in England.

'What am I doing here?' he asked himself. He was now a far cry from the man who had boasted to his friends, 'Dangers, what danger? I spit in the eye of danger.'

The sound of crushing silk that he had heard a number of times in recent days brought him out of his thoughts as the cage hit the twelve level station. The chain door lifted and a sweet sickly smell filled the cage and Matt's lungs. The ground in front of him ran red with blood mixed with water, frothing slightly as it ran back into the shaft and down to the sump. Matt gagged at how fresh spilt human blood smelt so sweet. The pikanins were washing out the train carriage with a hosepipe where the initial conflict had begun.

'What has been going on here?' screamed Biltong at some team leaders who were busy organising the clear up.

It struck Matt how this place did indeed work on fear and intimidation. The board would intimidate the mine manager, who would in turn intimidate the mine captain and shift bosses, who would then intimidate the white miners and other general workers like Biltong, who would in turn all join in to intimidate the black man. The black man was bottom of the ladder and considered the perpetrator of all things that went wrong in the mine – at least in the eyes of the whites who were, in their own estimation, nothing short of demigods. Truly, negative words and actions initiating from the business head caused a deep, dark rot, a cancerous infection that spread fear and selfish indifference and a culture of blame throughout the business. Matt had concluded by now that he would really need to keep his wits about him and engage his brain properly for the first time in years. His very survival may depend on it. He was not going to be put off by the racists that he now worked with, he came for money and nothing was going to stop him fulfilling his yearning for a better life, no matter what the price might have to be in the short-term.

'What has been going on?' Biltong demanded again.

'The two tribes, Baas.' said Natu nervously, a team leader from the Xhosa tribe.

It transpired that a black, who had been drinking the night before, had taken someone else's place in the mine train carriage, even though he was not entitled to do so since he worked less than a mile from the shaft. The aggrieved black, a Zulu, had argued for several minutes before he calmly pulled out a blade and slashed the man's throat where he sat. A friend of the dying man then picked up a metre long drill steel and bludgeoned the perpetrator to death with it. Then an all-out fight ensued between the factions among the twenty-four men present.

'Three men were dead before the arrival of the security forces and several had severe knife and bludgeon injuries. The security forces then let the dogs go into the thick of the fighting.' Natu continued to describe how one dog followed the command to disarm and disable, which really meant getting its massive jaws around a throat and crushing the victim's windpipe. However, on this occasion the young Zulu warrior was used to fighting the local wildlife of his homeland and managed to slit the dog's throat before it had applied deadly pressure. He had then staggered around for a few seconds, blood gushing from his wound, before he was shot in the face by the dog's handler. The security forces had shot eleven men in all at close range with a twelve bore; five fatally and the others had wounds ranging from potentially fatal to disabling, having been shot in both legs.

Matt sat against the sidewall of the tunnel almost losing his earlier breakfast of vetkoeks and coffee as the details came out. Other ears must have it heard it all many times before and seemed indifferent to the whole episode. Matt realised he was still really a boy in view of what his new mining colleagues seemed to take as typical events. He felt that he was now trapped in a man's world of extreme violence and danger, a nightmare scenario that overwhelmed the young English coal miner.

No punch-up outside the local chip shop, or five rounds of Queensbury rules in the miner's welfare car park after a few pints on a Saturday night, could have prepared him for what he was experiencing now and he trembled violently. As the last of the blood and water was swept down the shaft in front of him, the sound of crushing silk filled his ears. He climbed aboard the wet mine train for just another day on number six shaft.

Chapter 5

Four weeks later

Hard rock gold mines were very different to collieries in the Midlands coalfields and there was no need for supports other than rock bolt supports in the tunnels – metal rods not unlike shepherd's crooks were hammered into cement-filled drill holes about one point eight metres deep and left to set. It was usually below the level of fifteen hundred metres that mesh wiring and cable tensions between the roof bolts were used to strengthen the tunnels, which could be over-sprayed with fine cement if the ground was particularly unstable. Matt asked his shift boss, Grayling, why the tunnels that they were examining on sixteen level had this higher level of support since the surrounding rock was stable and they were only just over thirteen hundred metres underground.

'There is a huge fault line that runs away to the west for about four kilometres to the shaft that I am told is high value, gold bearing ore, but the ground becomes very unstable when it is approached. Although we won't be going anywhere near it, it is actually outside the mine boundary into land that belongs to the Shona, who are pretty fearsome warriors when roused. Those kaffirs believe in the land's spiritual value, they are their ancestral lands for which many of their forefathers died fighting Queen Victoria's Empire troops.'

'I see,' said Matt, 'that red area that was on the mine map in Meneer Symington's office.'

'I thought I told you not to ask about that,' replied Grayling, 'but yes, that is right. Brandy is not the only thing that makes Symington drunk. He is drunk with greed and the pursuit of wealth, that is why he is willing to sacrifice anything and anyone to get it.' Grayling pondered a minute before adding, 'I have been in mining all my life and I know one thing, those who love money will never have enough of it, the pursuit of wealth without a focused reason for it, kills a man's soul. And I am reminded that the scriptures say that those who remove the treasures of the earth will not be counted blameless. I long for another career, but with a wife and four children that is only a dream and the fact that I failed to matriculate from school means that in the modern South Africa, this is as good as it gets for me.'

'Surely you can do something else if you really put your mind to it?' Matt responded, aware of the irony of him coming halfway across the world to seek his fortune in a place that appeared to be full of intrigue and mystery, where those already doing the work, like Grayling, could think of nothing worse to do for a living. He was reminded of the grass and it not being so green and promised himself that he would stick to his original plan; he was not here for the growing and tending he was only here for the reaping.

Grayling continued, 'My family owns a garage and workshops and my two brothers Janie and Marcus work there, but my fingers are too fat for the work of a mechanic, look.' He displayed fingers that were short and resembled thick Boston sausages. 'My youngest brother Clint works on four level, he like me never matriculated and he is a bit slow but he is not stupid like the others say about him. I look after him and he is always at the production parties where there is lots of free booze and the best food, they have one at the end of the month. I make sure that he gets an invite.'

'You have a close family then?' Matt asked, as he sat down on the ground to take off his wellington boots and pour out the sweat.

'We are all Christians in our family. My father is a lay minister and we love our country. Our forefathers fought and died for this country and that is why we will not give it back to the black man. You see we earned it by our blood and we own everything by the fact that nothing of value was here until we came, that is the Dutch I am talking about not the pommies who stole it from us in the Boer War.'

'But isn't it a fact that there was always gold here, which means that the only value that was here was the gold and that it belongs to the natives really?' Matt enquired.

'These kaffirs have been wandering around after their animals on the top of this gold for tens of thousands of years and other than the outcrops on the surface they would never have done anything with it or have known anything was even there,' Grayling replied in an angry tone. 'They do not care about gold, they care about cattle and wives and tribal warfare and having more little kaffirs to keep them in their old age. The Zulus and Xhosa hate each other more than the Afrikaner hates either of them and that is why they kill and murder each other. No man can kill a man like a black man.'

'Yes, Meneer Symington said that to me too and I didn't understand it then and still don't think I do,' said Matt. 'But that fight on twelve level four weeks ago really shook me up, they seem to kill each other without guilt or remorse, like it is expected that they should.'

Grayling looked pensive for a few moments before answering, 'You have to understand they are native warriors. If they fight and one does not die, they fear that their opponent will come in the night and murder them anyway, so when a fight starts the death of one of them is inevitable.'

'But there has to be some good in them,' Matt asked in a hopeful manner. 'They seem to be okay with me, although I don't really trust them, if I am being honest. I think they don't quite understand why the whites on the mine treat me differently.'

'Oh, they understand perfectly well. They know that once you have been here a while you will hate them just as much as the locals do. You are just another white man, only from a different tribe.'

'I don't believe that. They have already given me a special name that I think means something to them. They know that I don't hate them. I feel what they are feeling in many ways, as everyone has been very unkind to me since I arrived here.'

Grayling, seemingly puzzled, asked with interest, 'Oh really? So what is this special name they have given you?'

'Well, I'm still trying to learn Fanagalo, but they call me Mulungu all the time.'

Grayling erupted into fits of laughter, his podgy face and hands turned a pinkish colour as he bent over double. 'You dumb pommie bastard!' He panted as he struggled to control his breathing then burst out with, 'Mulungu means white shit.'

Matt, now embarrassed and angry, said, 'Well they call you lot rock spiders that steal their inheritance.'

Grayling's laughter stopped abruptly and he said, with menace in his eyes, 'You would be wise never to use that term in front of any Afrikaner.'

Matt, back-pedalling, quickly replied, 'I think you are right though, they would never have the sense to get this gold out on their own.'

These words appeased Grayling who retorted, 'You see, it is obvious when you really think about it. Without the white man Africa would just be ignorant savage tribes fighting over waterholes and ant hills. It is the white man who rules the world, the blacks are merely the hewers and carriers of wood, as our minister says in his sermons.'

'Is that the same minister that Mrs Van dar Westheizen speaks about?' Matt asked.

'Yes. She and her husband are group leaders in our church. Do you know her? She is a mostly godly woman; she treats everyone kindly and knows how to keep the blacks in their place. As a local magistrate you can always count on her to give them long sentences of bread and water whilst they repent of their sins.'

Matt considered Grayling's comment in light of his few dealings with her. Like she had ever known simple bread and water he thought as he recalled visiting her house to pick up the keys for his mine accommodation. A house with three full-time servants and a full-time cook, a twenty-five metre swimming pool and a large Mercedes on the drive. 'You're my only friend then on the mine,' said Matt.

'I am not your friend and do not ever tell anyone that. I just do not like the way that they treat some whites, you may be only one rung up the ladder from the kaffir but you are still a white man and that makes a difference, although only slightly in your case. If you ever mention that we had this conversation, or any others that we might have in the future, I will not only deny it but hand you over to Venter. And I can tell you that he is the devil incarnate. He will make your life a misery and you would stand no chance with him and that is why I volunteered to take you, to give you a fighting chance here. And some have questioned why I did that. I told them, to save face, that I wanted the pleasure of being the one that would make you squirm off back to England like a whelping dog. So this is your chance. Don't mess it up and do exactly what I tell you.' Grayling smiled in a friendly and honest manner, then continued, 'I will make sure that you get invited to the production party next month, you deserve it. You have made great advances with your tunnels. Is that because of Joseph or you, you crafty pommie?'

'A bit of both I think. Joseph is good guy, his heart is in the right place.'

Grayling looked him in the eyes and said, 'He is a kaffir.'

'I know.' Matt finished Grayling's words, 'I'll watch my back. But he's different.'

Grayling's attention was caught by a piece of rock he accidentally stood on, causing him to stumble slightly. 'That is strange,' he said, kneeling down to pick at a piece of rock about the size of half a brick, hanging off the sidewall.

'What is it?' asked Matt, watching Grayling wet the piece of rock with water from his bottle.

'This looks like . . . no, it cannot be.' Grayling, now in a world of his own, examined the rock with the light from his cap lamp.

'Grayling!' came a shout from some metres down the tunnel. 'What are you doing here?' demanded Symington as his rotund frame came into the light from the two standing together.

'Nothing Meneer,' he replied. 'We were just on the way to west seven cross cut to see what we need to start blasting next month.'

'What is that you have in your hand?' asked Symington.

'I think it is . . .' Grayling put out his hand.

Symington rapped Grayling's hand with his silver-knobbed cane, which made him drop the rock. He pulled his hand back close to his side as he tried not to cry out in pain.

'Like a kaffir in a sweet shop are you not Grayling? Always got your fingers in some jar that does not concern you. Go away, and take that pommie with you before Venter gets here with the geologist. I cannot stand to be in the presence of more than one pommie at the same time.'

'Yes, Meneer.'

Grayling turned around and walked humbly away, Matt followed, wondering what it was about this place to make men treat each other in such a way.

The dull thwack of Symington's cane as he laid it across the back of his pikanin, Sela – who had done no more than dare to lift his eyes and look into the malefactor's face as he handed him his water – was the last sound they heard as they left the tunnel.

Chapter 6

'Berriman, you pommie bastard, how long are you going to keep me waiting?' shrieked Symington as the hapless geologist and the shift boss, Venter, Symington's whipping boy, turned the corner from seven west cross cut tunnel. 'Coetzee has been looking for you Berriman. I think he is going to eat your balls about the grade on six east six, that is if you have any left by the time we have finished today.'

'I cannot control the grades,' whined Berriman, 'I can only show you where I think the gold is and keep sampling it for grade. I never put it there; it's been there for millions of years.'

'Don't get smart arsed with me Berriman,' snorted Symington, 'I pay you to find the gold, so find it.'

'Why are we on sixteen level? The gold is almost exhausted here!' exclaimed Berriman. 'We need to be looking at twenty-two level. Look at this reef drive tunnel wall here, it has run into a fault, there is no gold here. I can confidently say that.'

'Really? I was just about to be shown something by a shift boss, one that failed to even matriculate from school and I know what he was going to say. It is something that you have failed to spot, look at that footwall, where I have washed with my water bottle. What conglomerate is it Berriman?'

Symington grew increasingly sarcastic. He had, somehow, gained his mine manager's certificate, but still had little understanding of the realities of mining. He did, however, enjoy its profits with reckless, illegal gambling that showed a wealth beyond the apparent size of his salary. He turned to his sidekick, 'Venter, tell this pommie what it is we are looking at, as he seems to be a bit unclear.'

'Pommies, rooi necks all of them,' said Venter, 'weak, insipid, bullying colonialists and . . .'

'Venter,' interrupted Symington. 'I told you to tell Berriman what conglomerate we have here, not a Boer history lesson.'

'I know what it looks like, but it cannot be.' Berriman interjected, trying to claw back some authority, 'And I will tell you why, that rock is at least a thousand feet beneath us and it is not the footwall of the Carbon Leader, it's just a scar, a blemish in the rock layer. The stone marbling just makes it appear like the CL, but it's not.'

Symington exploded, thrusting his cane millimetres from Berriman's face and screaming, 'You are wrong, you are wrong!' He then began clawing at the footwall with his hands, removing the fine dirt to expose the hard rock. 'All that education at Oxford, or other shithole of a university you went to, was money pissed down a drain. Where is your faith, man?'

'In science,' Berriman replied smugly handing him his scraping tool.

Symington looked intently at Berriman before saying, 'I will get Venter to wipe that smile of your face in a minute. Here, do this, kaffir,' he snapped at Sela. 'This is kaffir's work.'

His breathless, bloated frame lent against the tunnel sidewall blowing like a steam train. His minor exertions left his flabby physique red-faced, with beads of sweat dripping from his chin. He proceeded to berate Sela for lack of effort, raising his cane above shoulder height in a threatening manner, only he had no energy to deliver a blow so Sela was off the hook, at least until Symington got his breath back.

'Come on dig, kaffir, dig!' shouted Venter. 'We have not got all day.'

'That's enough,' said Berriman. 'We only need a couple of feet clearing.'

'That is comma five, kaffir,' Venter said to Sela. 'These pommies do not understand metric.'

'Now wash it down,' Symington demanded.

'Get out the way!' Venter pushed Sela to the sidewall. 'I will take a piss on it.'

No one said anything, astounded at the man's genitalia; Venter was always keen to show off his obvious attraction for the females. Symington, feeling somewhat belittled, made light of it by calling Venter a braying stallion.

'I am not sampling it if Venter pisses on it,' declared Berriman.

'Sela, go fetch a bucket of water from the stand pipe down there,' Symington barked.

On Sela's return Berriman was still protesting that the rock formation was a blip and they were wasting their time, his face was tense with exasperation as he said, 'Let's go to twenty-two level and that new reef drive at east seventeen cross cut.'

'I get it,' Symington couldn't resist a dig. 'You fear the possibility that this could be the Black Reef and that these kaffirs have put some sort of half-arsed curse on it, are you not Berriman?'

'No,' the geologist snapped back confidently, 'it is just I have seen terrible things happen when these blacks start their voodoo and black magic stuff. I remember there was this women who came . . .'

'Oh shut it, Berriman,' Venter interrupted, looking at Berriman with complete disdain. 'We are not interested in your black man voodoo, back from the dead, power stories. The only good kaffir is a dead one anyway.'

'So what is that then?' asked Symington, pointing to the footwall with his lamp beam that reflected back as bright as daytime running lights.

'It's only a scar, a patch,' said Berriman.

Sela was now extremely nervous and took several steps back down the tunnel.

'Yes. You see Berriman, even this dumb kaffir knows what this is,' Symington broke off a small piece of black rock with grey pebbles and what appeared to be iron pyrite attached to it, the size of shotgun pellets. He brought the piece of rock up to eye level within his light, the reflection was almost blinding in comparison with the darkness of the surrounding tunnel and lit up his beaming face like a disco ball.

Sela, now fifty yards away, cried out, 'Umshlope injan wen as heffa.'

Venter gave chase, 'I will kill you, you kaffir bastard!' he shouted, but Sela was gone in a second.

Symington stood transfixed as he eyed the rock and almost drooled. 'Forget him Venter. We have much more important things to deal with than native witchcraft and half-cocked tribal spiritual ancestry bullshit.'

'Did you hear what he said? White dogs you will die! Black bastard.'

'You inbred, forget him. He will get his later. I will have my Boys' Brigade search him out and administer some proper correction.'

The Boys' Brigade were a group of savage men of the Basotho tribe who would do Symington's bidding for the price of a beer and a weekly half hour with the prostitutes in the mine's shabean. The Basotho Boys' Brigade fronted that establishment but Symington owned it lock, stock and barrel. He was not really interested in the extortion that took place within it as long as it meant higher profits for him. Intertribal fighting broke out virtually every night over the high price of the alcohol and the poor quality of the disease-ridden young women who were paid less than fifty pence a time for anything-goes sex. The shabean, however, covered a deeper shame that only Symington and Coetzee knew about and that would prove to be their final undoing.

Berriman was now silent, like a student before his teacher, as he too looked at the rock in Symington's hand. His experience of twenty-seven years and his geology masters seemed meaningless because what he was looking at was not geologically possible according to every book he had ever read or the many papers he had studied over the years. The alleged value of the gold ore, or reef, was more mythical than geological. The legendary Black Reef – where it was alleged that black ore merged with a Carbon Leader – could not exist from a geological perspective because over one thousand metres of quartzite rock lay between two ore bodies. Therefore, it would have taken a cataclysmic event to cause the two to meet in an upward or downward fault plane. He smashed at the footwall with his rock hammer and picked up another piece. Symington now looked like a man drunk with love as he cherished his piece of the mythical Black Reef.

'I don't believe it. I have got it in my hand and I still don't believe it,' Berriman became excited about the serendipitous find.

'I want this assayed and graded before you go home tonight, Berriman.'

Berriman just nodded his head in acknowledgement.

'Venter, put a fence up at the end of this tunnel. I do not want any activity here, no one comes here, and I mean no one, do you hear me, Venter?'

Venter was already thinking about how much overtime and weekend work this was going to take. All to be undertaken in secrecy and illegally, since no blasting was allowed on Sundays.

'No one is to know of the find, not even Meneer Coetzee,' Symington growled. 'He was the biggest sceptic so we will not tell him about this find until we know the size and the extent of the ore body. Then we will surprise him with it.'

Berriman was still looking quizzically at the piece of rock in his hands.

'I don't think we should do that. Meneer gets very uptight about the grades and they are very low at the moment. He is getting a lot of pressure from the board that he keeps passing down onto me. This could really help him with his grade, he will be very grateful.'

'Not as grateful as I will be,' Symington replied in a conciliatory tone. 'Meneer will hear of it in good time and we want to be sure that we have our facts right. Another slip up from the geological department and I think that will be the final straw as far as your career with this company is concerned. Meneer Coetzee has already spoken to me about finding a replacement for your position Berriman; you would be wise to keep a low profile. You know what kind of low profile I mean. A little bit like we all keeping that secret about you and that weekend at Sun City and those showgirls and losing your month's salary in the casino. And may I remind you, Berriman, of the medical costs the company paid for you to have that condition cleared up that followed you back home and had to be covered up as a mine related infection?'

Berriman recalled the incident vividly. He had hoped it had slipped out of the memory of others two years post the event.

'I was drunk,' Berriman mumbled like a child caught in the act.

'We all have our little crosses to bear Berriman and Mrs Berriman has enough on her plate with that disabled child of yours. What is his name?'

'Sammy,' Berriman replied with a slow intake of breath.

'Yes, Sonny,' confirmed Symington.

'No, Sammy,' Berriman corrected.

'Whatever his name. Poor boy. The last thing your wife needs is you losing your job. So, do as I tell you and get those samples graded immediately.' His tone changed back to its usual bullish and arrogant self, his words rained down on Berriman who felt like a boxer's opponent on the ropes. 'Now get out of the mine and get me those results.'

Chapter 7

Six months in

'Where is my brigade?' shouted Symington.

'They are coming, baas,' said Sela, who had just spent the last forty minutes apologising to Symington for his outburst underground, saying that he was so afraid at finding the Black Reef that he just lost his mind. 'That is what it does to you, it sends you mad,' he'd pleaded, shaking and trembling uncontrollably, tears streaming down his face, whimpering as he buried his head in his hands, 'Only bad things will come from it baas, only bad things.'

As he finished speaking four of the blackest skinned men ever seen entered his offices with their hard hats removed and held in front of them, their eyes on the floor. 'Yes, baas?' they said in accord.

'How much money did you take at the shabean on Saturday night?'

'Err . . . four thousand rand' said Bantu, the team leader.

'Oh, really?' said Symington.

'No, I think it was four thousand four hundred,' said Nestu, the sidekick.

'Well, which one is it?' Symington barked. You could hear a pin drop in the palpable tension. Bantu lifted his eyes slightly to speak just as Symington's cane thwacked him across the face with a blow that was meant for his shoulder. Bantu winced but did not cry out; he was a Basotho and no stranger to pain. 'Did I say you could look at me, kaffir?' Symington enquired, now on a characteristic power trip.

Bantu's eye began to swell as he corrected his posture and said, 'It was definitely four thousand, sir.'

Symington took a deep breath and said quietly, 'You are my special boys. Do I not I look after you and give you the best of girls and a share of the takings?'

To a man they all said, 'Yes baas. You are very kind, always kind.'

'Take forty rand for you Bantu and give the rest to Sela. Count it Sela and put it into my drawer.' Symington spoke softly as if he was comforting a beaten child, 'Do you want to please your baas?'

'Yes we do baas. We are sorry baas,' they said.

'Look at me,' he said and they lifted their heads slowly and deliberately. 'Sela leave us.' Sela promptly left the office and Symington continued, 'Meneer Coetzee wants some fresh girls. As you know he always has the fresh ones before you make them work in the shabean, the clean ones that come to visit their husbands or family members who work here on the mine.'

'Yes baas. He likes the clean ones,' said Bantu.

Symington paused before saying, 'Did I not deny a pass for the sister of my pikanin to visit him a couple of months ago?'

'Yes, you did baas,' replied Bantu.

'Send a message that I have reconsidered and tell her she can come.'

'Sela will be pleased baas. He has not seen his sister in a long time.'

'Say nothing to Sela. I want it to be a big, big surprise. Now get out of my sight and back to work, except you Bantu. I want a word with you.' Bantu stood nervously as the others left the office. When they were finally alone Symington continued, 'Listen to me carefully, Bantu. When Sela's sister comes make sure that she is not aware that she stands in a queue with the local girls who want to work in the shabean as she comes through security. Then, when she has cleared security, take her straight to the mine flats and put her in Meneer Coetzee's overnight room. Tell her that her brother has special privileges and he will join her shortly. Do you understand Bantu?'

'I understand baas; I won't let you down baas.'

Symington thrust another twenty rand into Bantu's hands, 'Now go.'

***

'How long are you going to be, Temba?' asked Matt at the exact moment that Venter enquired the same of Sarah as he waited in his pickup outside her house.

'It is only half an hour till blasting time, nearly finished baas. They won't blast whilst we are still down here will they baas?' he asked Matt nervously.

'No, the mine law says that they cannot blast while anyone is still underground unless special ventilation equipment is in place.'

'I know baas. They say that six parts per million of gas will kill you, won't it baas?'

'Although, I would not be too trusting of anything shift boss Venter says,' stated Matt.

'No baas, me neither. I know mine law says we cannot blast on Sundays, but we do it all the time.'

Matt, taken aback by the comment, asked, 'We do?'

'Yes baas. When the grade is down we blast every day, only no one is supposed to know. Baas Venter said I had to get two crews for drilling and blasting next Sunday for this place, which is why he told me to barricade it today, baas.'

'Why, what is here?

'Not too sure, but something is not right about this place. They were talking about the Black Reef being here. Do you believe in the Black Reef, baas?'

'Nope. If I can touch, feel and see it I can believe in it. Anything else is not real, it's just another lump of stone like any other,' Matt was stopped by the sound of crushing silk and a momentary feeling of being in another place.

'So, you do not believe that this gold was the finger of Nunakulu's arm that he placed in the earth for the spiritual inheritance of the Shona people?' asked Temba.

'Sounds like bad juju bollocks to me.'

'No baas, please do not say that. It makes men crazy with gold fever and many bad things will happen if they take it out. I know for sure! I am glad I am going on my annual leave on Friday so I don't have to be here . . . Finished baas,' he said as he banged the last copper nail through a hole in the mesh and bent it over against the mine pole surface to hold it in place, completing the temporary fence.

'Right, let's go,' said Matt and they made their way towards the shaft; on accessing the station they found Biltong offloading locomotive rail tracks that were slung under the cage and heard the good news that he was going to be at least another forty minutes.

'Well,' Matt thought, 'at least there won't be any blasting as Biltong is the one who makes sure the shaft is clear before the late shift boss throws the switch.' So he relaxed in the banksman's cubicle and out of the cool air that went down the shaft into the deeper levels.

***

'It's warm tonight,' said Sarah as she jumped into Venter's pickup, bursting out of her ill-fitting red blouse and cream coloured skirt that looked no wider than a belt.

'Yes, it is,' his passions roused by the sight of the leggy, buxom blonde sat next to him.

Sacky sacky music was playing full blast on the stereo. 'What's that shit?' she said, turning the knob to find another station.

'Get your hands off it!' shouted Venter. 'That is Afrikaner heritage, our ancestry that is.'

'Sounds like redneck, hillbilly shit to me.'

Venter was not amused but kept his cool as he had other plans and didn't want to put her off so early in the evening. He would get his own back later he thought, as he eyed the length of her legs from ankle to exposed thigh. Venter's one plan was to impregnate some conquest with his offspring. His own marriage had failed several years before because his wife did not conceive. He had definitely concluded there could not be anything wrong in his department. His activities were well-known in the town of Randstein, although they had not as yet produced the hoped-for fruit of his loins and he ignored his female offspring. He was desperate for a son whom he could teach to hunt, fish and drink like a true Afrikaner. Venter had also concluded that most of the women in Randstein were obviously barren, but he would keep trying and this bit of pommie skirt could prove to be just that opportunity. Though he had always hated pommies the females were fair game and the only female that he found abhorrent was the black variety.

After two hours of drinking Venter's arousal had reached fever pitch. The young, voluptuous English flower that sat before him could not only drink as much as he did but was leaving him in no uncertain terms as to how the evening would conclude. Sarah had deliberated briefly on her actions as a married woman and concluded that her husband had become a slave to his work in the six months of being in the country, although those long hours scarcely brought in enough money to keep her in clothes and make up. Also, that Matt was so exhausted at the end of the day that she rarely had her needs serviced in the manner she would have liked. She decided she had never really loved Matt anyway and concluded that this trip to Africa was little more than an extended holiday which had failed to live up to its expectations. Justified by those thoughts she put her hand into Venter's groin with a shallow smile that signalled it was time to leave.

***

'I thought we would never get out,' complained Matt to Biltong as he stepped out of the cage. 'Two bloody hours I have been sat on that station. What took you so long?'

Biltong thought, a bit of this and that but that is the least of your problems. Although complicit in Venter's schemes, he hated him with a vengeance since his own son's marriage had been wrecked by the man's unrelenting urges. He will get his one day, he pondered, but until that day he would have to bite his tongue since one word from Venter to Coetzee and his final thirty-six months of work before retirement would come to a sudden end. But, he vowed, one day he would see the sun go down on that bastard for the last time. He said to Matt, 'Best get home. Your wife will be wondering where you are.'

'No, she'll be alright. She was going to some ladies book club tonight. She won't be back until about ten.'

Biltong said nothing and put the horseshoe safety bracket on the shaft gates as Matt walked towards the change house.

Arriving home around seven to a house in darkness Matt walked into the kitchen to see if there was a meal in the oven. Eleven hours underground in the heat and dust and the rigours of kilometres of walking had taken their toll. He had stuffed some polony sandwiches down him at the midpoint of the day, which he had quickly put together at half five that morning and, although better than nothing, they had turned slimy with the heat by the time he'd come to eat them. Ravenous, he scoured both fridge and oven but found no meal, only a note saying, 'Didn't have time to do any dinner, got to rush book club starts in an hour Sarah x'. He slammed the fridge door. 'Ungrateful bitch, she has nothing to do all day but keep herself entertained, do a bit of washing and cook a meal,' he said out loud, as though a sympathetic audience was listening.

***

Venter was pulled back onto the flatbed of the pickup truck by an obviously unsatisfied Sarah. He had laid out some blankets on the plywood surface for the anticipated ten-minute romp, which was now into forty-five minutes and Venter had more than met his match. As he was trying to prise away her hand grasping his appendage she said, 'I thought you were real man?'

There was a stunned silence before Venter retorted, 'Get off you bitch!'

'You're just like all the rest,' Sarah said sarcastically. 'Lots of promise, big stories, you have never had a man like me and then that pitiful effort. Matt said you were just a talking cock and he was right.'

Venter pulled her by the hair off the back of the pickup and kicked the dark red African dust into her face. While she was coughing and spluttering he got into the cabin, started the truck and drove away, leaving her three miles outside town, behind a rundown, boarded up diner that had been closed for several years. The locals had called it Stollie's Place, then old man Stollie was shot dead by some kaffirs in a stolen pickup, apparently in a robbery. They were never caught, had seemed just to vanish into thin air. Symington, as sole heir and executor of his Uncle Leonard Stollie Symington's estate, gave a tearful tribute at the funeral while the mining rights were being worked out by his Johannesburg solicitors. Stollie's one hundred and ten acre site was now a bolt hole for Symington should his latest scheme not work out.

***

'What bloody time do you call this?' Matt demanded as a rough looking and windswept Sarah walked through the front door, 'and what's all that dust in your hair?'

'I got caught in one of those little cyclones that you see from time to time and it covered me with dust. You know, like that one we watched the other weekend in the garden.'

Matt recalled the event, 'Blimey, it must have been quite a big one.'

'Yes, it was,' she adjusted the seam on her skirt to face the front.

'Have you been drinking? Your eyes are all bloodshot.'

'A little, but it's this bloody dust in my eyes.'

Matt disappeared into the kitchen and came back with a bowl of warm water and a flannel and began bathing her eyes. For a second the tenderness of the moment struck Sarah's heart, but it was fleeting as she assured herself that her actions earlier in the evening were justified on the basis of her need for a real man, although Venter had stumbled at the first fence. Some stallion he turned out to be, she thought, that's rumours for you. Then she kissed the end of Matt's nose in a childlike manner.

Chapter 8

The following morning Symington was in his office. 'Where is Venter?' he demanded of Sela.

'I don't know, baas. I haven't seen him this morning.'

'Shut it kaffir,' said Venter, pushing Sela out of the way as he walked into the office. 'Morning Meneer. Sorry I am a bit late, had a bit of a rough night.'

'I'd rather not know. Sela, don't just stand there. Get me and Venter some coffee and shut the door behind you.'

Symington leant towards Venter from the other side of his mahogany desk and beckoned him a little closer, 'Who are we going to use to mine that Black Reef as none of these Shona are going to have anything to do with it?'

'But it is not really the Black Reef is it, Meneer? Hasn't Berriman come back with the samples and it is only a scar?' somewhat surprised at the request.

'Am I the only one with any vision?' barked Symington. 'You of all people Venter should know that I am not a man who runs away from this African witchcraft and voodoo nonsense. I do not care what they call it, it is valuable ore that may run into a gold bar the further we get down and we are going to have to drive a winze down to get it as we cannot possibly access it from the lower level without going outside the mine boundary.'

'Going outside the boundary never bothered us before,' replied Venter.

'You would be wise to keep your mouth shut about that Venter. You didn't do badly out of it as I recall. There were a few questions as to how a shift boss could afford a forty thousand rand, deluxe pickup truck. Rumours I had to stamp out on your behalf. So, you believe it is the Black

Reef then?' Symington asked, thinking, a winze, it is slow going downhill and especially dangerous through that fault plane. That must have been a big one if the Carbon Leader has been thrown so far up it has touched the Black Reef.

'Like you Meneer, I don't care what they call it if we make some money,' Venter replied.

'Play your cards right Venter and do exactly what I tell you and it could be the last time that we need to work on this shithole of a mine or any other. And if we can conjure up a few fatal accidents Meneer Coetzee will need some allies to prevent him doing some jail time for negligence. That could get me my father's mining rights back, at a keep him out of jail price.'

'You have it all worked out don't you, Meneer? I wish I had your mind for business,' Venter said admiringly.

'You do not though, Venter, you are just a Boer farm boy with pig shit between your ears and toes.' Venter's face dropped, liked a spanked child's and Symington, realising that his ally's sensibilities were hurt and that he would need him fully on his side for the fraud, extortion, blackmail and possible murder he was planning – although, he pondered, it is not really murder as they are only kaffirs – continued in a conciliatory tone, 'But great things are grown out of pig shit and you cannot help what you were born into. The facts are, Venter, that many are born into a poor and difficult situation, but the truth is Venter, they do not have to stay there. Do you want to stay in the pig shit Venter or do you want to be like me, a man of success? Forget all that religious nonsense that Grayling spouts off in the change house about the weak inheriting the earth and all that. It is the strong that survive Venter. Those who use their mind and elevated positions to take from those who are not strong enough to keep a hold of it. What have you taken recently that did not directly belong to you Venter? Something that you could take by force, something that you wanted but was held by someone else and yet you knew you could take by force. Notice, I said held by someone else Venter. Do you know why? Because we can only own something if we have the power to keep it. If anything can be taken from us we don't own it, we only have temporary custody.'

'Oh, I see . . .' Venter pondered. 'A bit like life, because anyone can die at any time or any day. Especially on this mine.' He believed his comment to be a wise and considered remark.

Symington fumed but kept it hidden. He put his hand into his desk drawer and retrieved his nineteen millimetre Grand Power K100, Slovak revolver. Venter's eyes brightened at the sight.

'Oh, you like your revolver don't you? It was your father's, was it not? Do you know what this really is Venter?' pointing it at Venter's face, who said nothing. 'It is power. You are right, any day, any time we can die, the difference in this situation is that I hold the power. The power to let you live or to blow your stupid Boer brains all over the maps on the wall behind you.' He continued with menace in his eyes, 'At this moment in time Venter, I am god and you are in my hands completely and the only way you can change that is if you can take this gun from me before I pull the trigger and it splits your skull like a ripe peach.' Symington cocked the hammer on the revolver.

'Menneeerrrr!' shrieked Venter.

'Shut up,' said Symington, placing the hammer back down carefully. 'I am only making a point.'

'I see, I see,' Venter replied nervously, relieved.

'Do you really see Venter? Make no mistake, it is only the power that the kaffirs believe we have that keeps them from overrunning and taking everything from us. Like they did to my family in Rhodesia.'

'You mean Zimbabwe, Meneer?'

'No!' Symington shouted as he banged the drawer shut having placed the gun back. 'It will only ever be Rhodesia to those who built that country, like my father. Venter, I will tell you something, one day very soon these kaffirs will realise, as they did in Rhodesia, that this is their land, their inheritance and the best thing that we can do in the meantime is get our share – and I mean a big share – and get out of this country. That is why we are going to get that Black Reef. It is ours Venter. We have the power don't you see? And we have to use it whilst we have it.'

'Yes, I see. You're right, Meneer, these bastard kaffirs get whiter every day and there is nothing more dangerous than a kaffir who thinks like a white man.'

'Stop there, Venter, the very thought of a black ever being able to think like a white man is abhorrent to me. They are just animals with brute instinct, like it says in the Bible, hewers of wood and carriers of water. But they hunger for power and will slit each other's throats for any kind of advantage.'

'Coffee, Baas,' Sela came through the door with two mugs of steaming coffee.

'Where is my china mug?' asked Symington.

'Err, sorry Baas, it got broke. It fell off the sink top when I was washing yesterday, but this is a new one I got from the mine store for you on my way in early this morning, Baas.'

Sela put down the coffee and stood waiting for further instructions. Symington stood up and moved slowly towards Sela with his cane behind his back. As Symington raised his cane Sela covered his head and face as best he could.

'Put your hands down!' screamed Symington.

'No baas! No baas, please!' cried Sela.

'Take it like a man.'

'Please, baas. No, baas.'

Sela cowered down on his haunches in submission to the inevitable hiding. Symington landed stroke after stroke on Sela's hands, splitting the skin over his knuckles and with each stroke the sound echoed off the office walls. Symington turned to Venter and grinned as he beat Sela towards to the office door, 'You see Venter, power, that is the only thing these kaffirs understand.'

Sela, gripped the door knob with both bleeding, bruised and swollen hands and winced with pain as there was no strength left in them and the swelling was making them unusable.

'You did not answer my question, Venter,' said Symington as he sat down on his chair, breathless from his exertions.

'Well, between you and me, although the other shift bosses know already, that I had that pommie's wife last night. So I suppose that was the last time I took something that didn't belong to me and yes, you are right, I took it because I could. The pommie couldn't keep a hold of it could he?'

'In a way you are right. But, I reserve my power for taking financially. You need to start thinking with your head, Venter, and not your manhood, if you want to achieve something useful.'

'I know you are right Meneer, but I am getting older, nearly fifty-four, and I do not have a son to carry on my name.'

'And you are very proud of your family name are you not Venter?'

'Yes Meneer. All my brothers have children and I have none and I am the eldest. It should be my bloodline. Do not get me wrong, Meneer, I like having the power I have over women, but it is a son I really want.'

'What do you think the pommie will do when he finds out? And he certainly will, as well you knew when you told the other shift bosses. They will be falling over themselves to deliver that good news to the pommie.'

'What can he do, Meneer? He is half my height and weight. He will probably crawl back to England with his salt peel between his legs and pretend it never happened.'

'Do not underestimate the pommies, Venter. They have proved to be calculating and extremely proud fighting men when it suits them. It was their tenacity, and thirty miles of salt water, that prevented the whole of Europe coming under the rule of Nazis like Meneer Coetzee in the second world war. Anyway, I have other plans for the pommie. How much is he earning?' He moved away from his desk and looked at the mine plan on the wall.

'Well, he should be earning around four thousand rand per month but we have been holding back on the measurements at month end and splitting the difference between the shift bosses. He does not know, not very bright that pommie.'

So, Symington reflected, he will be struggling for money then.

'His slut of a wife was complaining to me that she never has the money to entertain herself at the mine social club the way that she would like, or to go clothes shopping to Jo'burg, not that she keeps her clothes on long enough to appreciate them,' Venter jeered.

Symington did not respond to Venter's wit but just looked pensive and simply said, 'Good.'

Chapter 9

Two weeks later

'Watch out!' cried Dirk Grayling, shaking his cap lamp for emphasis as the mine car, full of broken ore, thundered past Matt as he walked down east fourteen cross cut. It just missed him as he had stumbled only seconds before on a loose rail spike, forcing him to lean towards the sidewall and the mine car brushed the sleeve of his overall. The sound of crushing silk filled his ears.

Matt shook the sound from his head, corrected his stance and yelled, 'Bloody hell, Dirk, what's going on?'

'I don't know where that mine car came from,' Dirk said with concern. 'I was only at the shaft station a moment ago and the mine cars were all standing and there were no locomotives around to push them.'

'Well, somebody bloody pushed it for it come down the tunnel like that, didn't they?' Matt was tired from a poor night's sleep as Sarah had kept him up all night being sick.

'I will ask some questions later. Are you sure you're okay?' he held out his water bottle for Matt to take a drink.

'Yes. Sorry Dirk, I'm a bit cranky this morning. Finished really late again yesterday and my wife has some bug or other and kept me up all night.'

Dirk knew about Venter's antics and tried not to look into Matt's eyes in case his own gave the game away. Dirk was in no way complicit with Venter, he virtually hated the man who brought such shame to the name of the Christian Afrikaners. Dirk considered that Matt would know soon enough, but he was not the one that was going to tell him. He felt for Matt who seemed to have no friends, was alienated by the whites as a pommie foreigner and mistrusted by the blacks for being a white man, and whose own wife was even stabbing him in the back.

'Matt, take this, you may need it at some point.'

'What is it?' Matt took the paper from Dirk's hand.

'It is the number for my Dad's church; he is senior pastor at the Meadows Community Church. They have an open day next month.'

'No thanks Dirk, I am not into any kind if religion. If I can touch it I can believe it, that's my ethos. And what has God ever done for me? I have got this far in life on my own and I don't need anyone else. Just me and my wife, we are okay. It's tough at the moment but I'm sure that I'll start earning some good money soon and things will get sorted out between us. Anyway Dirk, I am not being funny but all that church stuff is just a crutch for the weak isn't it?' he said, with a deep sigh, however the faraway look in his eye was less than convincing.

'That may be true in the minds of some but a crutch is not a bad thing to have around when you have two broken legs is it? And it only takes a turn in life for it to become very fractious. I meant to tell you that you should not stay late at the behest of Venter. I am your shift boss, not Venter, and have you ever been paid for all those extra hours you have been doing?'

Matt thought, 'Well, no. I thought if I helped Venter out he might take it a bit easier on me.'

'Venter has another agenda and it has nothing to do with making any kind of friend out of you any time soon. So you can drop that thought right now. Venter's kind are a scourge on our society, dim-witted and bull-headed racists that have not changed for centuries. Men like Venter believe that there is still a Boer war going on, only it is not solely against the British but against everyone who is not a Boer

Afrikaner or who do not think as they do. Brute beasts they are and the coming judgement will be just.'

Taken aback by the last comment Matt asked, 'Judgement! What do you mean, judgement?'

'Can't you see what is going on around you? These blacks are not going to put up with this apartheid forever you know. There will be a day of reckoning and on that day the likes of Venter will get what is coming to them.'

The men walked down the tunnel for a short distance before Matt said, 'Interesting that you say that. I heard that Venter, a few years ago, had a black Zulu team leader tied up on the face at blasting time and it was Meneer Symington's Boys' Brigade who did it.'

'Like I said, the judgement is coming and those who give the orders are as guilty as those who do the acts, and in fact even more so. As for the so called Boys' Brigade, they do what they do for Symington out of fear and no other reason. Given the opportunity they would open him up with their tribal knives like the big, fat, bloated hippo that he is.'

Dirk and Matt broke off, feeling that they had just indulged in a conversation that was unrealistic and improper, like two children engaged in a fantasy of revenge.

'Anyway, Meneer Symington has asked to see you at the end of the shift. I don't know what he wants but I don't think I will be your shift boss anymore. You may be working for him directly, which is very strange. Just watch your back, I cannot protect you anymore and never be alone if you can help it. Remember, no man can kill a man like a black man and that is no way for a man to find himself suddenly in the hands of God.'

'I have already learnt that,' said Matt. 'That time one black guy slit another's throat for sitting in his place on the mine train. What kind of craziness is that? It's barbaric.'

Dirk smiled wryly, 'No, it is Africa and it will never change. You can always tell when a Zulu has killed a man as he takes the eyes with him, believing that the last image he saw is retained in his eyes and it will find him out.'

'You know what, I believed that this kind of darkness, with the witchcraft and voodoo and stuff, was only in books and movies. We don't have this kind of stuff in England,' Matt said pensively. 'I mean, we get the odd crank who says that they have seen a ghost now and again and they are subjected to the ridicule that they probably deserve. But ever since I arrived here I have been hearing things and I am beginning to think that one of these bastard blacks have put some sort of curse on me.'

Dirk's attention was piqued, 'Really? Tell me what you have been hearing.'

'You'll laugh at me and say I am just a stupid pommie.'

'Okay, don't,' snapped Dirk, proceeding to walk further down the tunnel.

Matt really did want to discuss it with someone since he had experienced several strange events recently that were starting to worry him, but male pride got in the way and he felt he had no one he could trust with such things. The ridicule he received as the butt of coarse jests from the Afrikaners, virtually on a daily basis, had made him a little insular and non-communicative.

However, as Dirk was only a step ahead he asked, 'Do you really want to know?'

'I can guess. You won't be the first to hear and experience strange things down this mine, or any other like it. Many men lose their lives in these mines, around five hundred a year throughout the industry and the only difference between a South African gold mine and a slaughter house is the name above the door.'

'So you think it is the spirits of the dead that are bothering me then?' asked Matt with a nervous laugh.

'I don't know unless you tell me what you are experiencing, do I?'

'Well, it started the very first day I landed at the airport. I was woken by a sound like crushing silk, a sound I had never heard before but that I have heard a number of times since. In fact, just a few minutes ago when that mine car nearly took me out. And this is going to sound really weird and I cannot believe I'm actually going to say it, but when I am alone underground, like last week when you sent me to east nineteen cross cut to check on air and water supplies for next month's blasting, I heard someone calling my name. There was no one around and you know how far it is. No one works anywhere near there do they?' Matt waited for clarification that no one did.

'No, no one. The closest working place is about two kilometres away. How many times has this happened?'

'Too many to count. Am I going insane?'

'And what does the voice say?' Dirk wouldn't be drawn.

Matt sighed, 'It doesn't say anything, just calls my name and it happens more and more. Initially, I was really scared but after a while it just started to piss me off. Do you think it is one of these black voodoo curses?'

'No I don't think so. They always come very direct and they don't play with words. You would have suffered some physical side effects from a curse by now.'

Matt kicked the tunnel sidewall in frustration, annoyed with himself, 'Listen to what I'm saying! I don't believe in all this stuff.'

'Yes, I get what you said, if you can see it and touch it you can believe in it. Matt there are many things in this world that we cannot explain and I don't think that we can or should even try. Sometimes acceptance of that fact is the most sensible approach. Take God for example, many say that they cannot believe in a God that allows such suffering in the world, but if men knew the mind of God, then they would be God themselves knowing the beginning and the end of all things and then God would no longer be God. Simply because God does not act in any given situation in the way that they believe he should from a human perspective, they say there cannot be a God. But that point of view simply makes God a man like the rest of us, with no higher knowledge or outworking of purposes to an end or eventual conclusion. Do you understand what I mean?' Dirk asked Matt, looking straight into his eyes. Matt tried to digest all that discourse but it was clear to Dirk that he couldn't, 'Okay, put it like this, you believe in electricity don't you?'

'Well, I can see and touch it.'

'You can only see it when it sparks or lightning occurs. Most of the time you only know it is there by the effect it has on your TV or other electrical equipment.'

'Yes, I suppose.'

'Well, it is the same with the spiritual world. You only know it is there by the effect it has from time to time in our realm. Like when people make it cross over by using black magic and voodoo. The rest of the time it just works in the background, like electricity, no one notices it and if they do they just put such things down to coincidence and chance, or strange happenings with no real relevance.'

Now intrigued, Matt asked, 'How do you know all this?'

'I told you, my father is a senior pastor and for three years he was a missionary and our family lived on a mission in a Zulu village. I, like you, did not believe in that kind of stuff.'

Dirk pondered for a second, as if asking himself whether he should share some very personal, deep emotions and memories with Matt.

'I was eighteen years old, arrogant and, like you, knew it all and would never believe in anything I had not seen. Within two months I had seen so many strange things that I could no longer hold that view with any kind of honesty. I had witnessed people dying under voodoo curses and I had been visited many times by sangoma spirits in the night, often believing that I was dreaming, only to wake up and discover that the spirits were still in the room and they were real.'

'Bloody hell, I would have been scared shitless,' Matt took a depth breath.

'I was. Eventually I had to confide in my father as they were starting to use sex magic against me. My own fault really, as I was constantly fantasising and then having dreams about having sex with the young black girls and I was enjoying it. But every time I indulged in it, it got more sickening and the sexual acts became almost animalistic and then in one dream there was a beautiful, lightly-coloured girl with whom I felt intensely in love. She turned to look at me as I was having sex with her from behind and said, "I love you too", in a voice that was male, deep and demonic. As I pulled away from her the scales fell from my eyes and I could see that she was in fact a hideously deformed demon.'

Matt, speechless for a moment, said, 'Go on.'

'My father was furious that I had let this situation go on for so long without telling him. The spirits had been incensed about the work he was doing with the villagers because many of them had become Christian. But they could not get to him as his faith was too strong, so they attacked the weakest member of his family, me, as the only nonbeliever. What their eventual plans were I did not know, but as I had come to love those dreams and the acts within them, it would probably not have been too long before I would have acted them out for real. The shame of that would have come back on my father and destroyed all his work in the village. Like I said, God knows the beginning from the end of all things and, although he allowed the situation to continue, he allowed it only long enough to fulfil his purposes in getting my attention in a way that I would never forget.'

'This is mad. You are really scaring me now. Do you think that's what happening to me?'

'Well, are you having dreams and seeing things like that?'

'Well no,' Matt replied in a thankful tone.

'Then it is not a voodoo curse or anything like that, but someone is trying to get your attention, if what you say is true,' Dirk replied.

Those words were more frightening to Matt than the stories that Dirk had just relayed. He had finally worked out that if it was not the darkness that was seeking his attention, then it must be the light and, not knowing anything about either, he was unsure which he would fear the most.

Chapter 10

Two weeks later

'Koos, is that you?' whispered Sarah as Venter sat in the change house, half-heartedly taking her call on the external mine phone, his hand bloodied from administering some punishment a few moments earlier as accuser, judge and jury on a young black lad apparently caught stealing bread from the compound kitchen. It could have been worse; Venter's party trick was to stick the tip of his razor sharp, Nazi bayonet knife into the victim's nasal passage, quickly flicking his wrist from right to left to severe the nasal septum. This caused the bulbous part to hang low and flap around awkwardly. Such events were followed by the statement, 'You see, that bit of skin is the only thing that stops you from being seen for what you really are, a baboon.' Venter smirked as put the phone to his ear, 'I did not expect to hear from you anytime soon.'

'Yes, well, I have forgiven you for that disgusting display of leaving me at the side of the road in the middle of nowhere a month ago.'

Venter grinned to himself as he recalled the incident. 'Well, what do you want?' he snapped, as his new pikanin, George, began to bathe his hands to clean off the blood. When George caught a bruised and tender area with the flannel, Venter gave him a look that said he would be getting a slap if he did it again.

'I need to speak to you,' she continued in a low voice.

'About what? I'm busy. What do you want really?'

'I need to speak with you,' Sarah insisted and lowered her voice even more as she looked around the local post office where she was using the public pay phone.

'Well, you are speaking with me,'

'No, in private,' she whispered.

'So, you have had second thoughts about wanting another slice of prime South African beef then?' Venter responded, fondling his manhood.

'Yes, something like that,' Sarah sighed.

'Well, meet me at the clubhouse in an hour.'

'I can't. Matt, is due home in an hour and a half and he will be expecting me to be at home as he thinks I'm ill.'

'Well, are you ill?' asked Venter, without concern.

Sarah had been unable to sleep for the third night running with acute vomiting. 'No I am not, but I need to see you and immediately. We have to sort something out.'

'Clubhouse then in an hour. And don't worry about the salt peel, I will make sure he doesn't get out of the mine till much later.'

'Okay,' she said, 'but outside the clubhouse not inside, we might be seen together.'

'A bit late for that. The only person who doesn't know that you are just another notch on my gear stick is that halfwit husband of yours,' Venter broke into laughter, 'and I am so looking forward to the look on his face when that one leaks out.'

'You bastard. Why I thought I could confide in you about our problem just shows what a mess I'm in. I should have known better, how many other girls have you left pregnant in your inability to control yourself?' she shouted angrily.

Venter's raucous and sarcastic laugh stopped immediately, 'What did you say?'

'I am pregnant, you dumb Boer,' she shouted down the phone.

'Is it a boy?' asked Venter instantly.

'What?' Sarah was stunned by his response. 'How the hell do I know? I am only one month gone. Why? What difference does it make to you? We are going to have to get rid of it and you're going to help me,' she said with venom in her voice.

Venter was silent.

'Koos Venter, are you there?' she demanded.

'Yes, yes. I am here. Just thinking, I mean shocked. Well, when I say shocked. Not that you're pregnant of course, I'm a full-blooded man with a sperm count that is off the planet, but let us not be hasty. I will be at the clubhouse in half an hour, be there.'

He slammed the phone down, pushing George aside as he went out into the yard and shouted to Biltong to come over. Venter stood in his white wellington boots and grey underpants, the afternoon sun hot on his hairy back.

'Yes! What do you want now?' Biltong asked.

'Keep a civil tongue in your head, or you will back shovelling shit at that half-arsed farm your dry old man keeps in the Free State and the only pension you will be having is the pods those filthy pigs won't eat, you plasse Boer. I bet you still have pig shit between your toes,' Venter menaced.

Biltong just looked Venter in the eye and thought, one day, one day.

'Are those mine rails underground yet?'

'No. There are still men underground. It will be another two hours, once we start slinging those below the cage to transport them down until we can wind men up the shaft.'

'Great. Start right now.'

'But what about the men?' Biltong asked in astonishment.

Venter turned around and began walking back into the change house. 'Is that pig shit just between your toes or also your ears? Just do as I tell you.' Venter proudly used Symington's insults as his own.

***

'Joseph, is the cage here yet?' asked Matt, 'I'm starving and need to get out and have some food.'

'No baas. They just rang for materials. I think they are going to be slinging rails.'

'What! There are still men down here. They have all night to do that, where is that banksman's phone?' Matt grasped the phone cubby at the shaft side and dialled the surface. 'Hello, Biltong. Pick up, Biltong. Pick up. He's not answering, I don't believe it and I'm bloody starving.'

***

Venter sat outside the clubhouse in his pickup truck as Sarah came over the manicured lawn and along the pathway of brushed sandstone slate and got in next to him. He broke the silence by asking if she was okay.

'Well, if you call being a month pregnant and the father not your husband being okay, then yes. What do you think? We have to get rid of this bastard thing inside of me!' she shouted.

Venter grabbed her by the throat, his massive hand engulfed her neck from chin to shoulders and he squeezed hard, 'Listen you pommie bitch. Any child of mine is no bastard, do you hear me?'

He continued to squeeze so tightly her windpipe made a cracking sound like a plastic water cup and the air stopped flowing into her lungs. Sarah made a gesture for Venter to stop. She understood the extreme physical power of the man and that any action on her part would have meant serious harm if she fought back. Venter let her go.

'Don't ever say that again, do you hear?'

'Yes, yes,' coughed Sarah. 'I'm sorry.' She let out a few crocodile tears for Venter's benefit, who just smirked.

'It is fine, don't worry, we will make plans. When we have found out what sex the child is we will make another plan for what we are going to do.' He felt all his Christmases may have come at once, what with the Black Reef and the money he would be getting from Symington's plan.

'But I can't keep it,' Sarah whined.

'Oh yes, you will. At least until we know whether I have a son or not. If I have a son we will bring it up together. You are a whore I know, but it will be a relationship of convenience. I will live my life as I do now and you will bring up our child until I take him on to train him how to be a man. I cannot believe my luck.' But, realising what he had said, quickly added, 'Another one to my quiver.' Venter threw his head back and looked up towards the dusky coloured, starlit sky and grinned.

'You have more children I take it then?' Sarah began sobbing, no crocodile tears now as the desperation of her predicament began to dawn on her.

'I am sure I have many. There are many men bringing up my children, unbeknown to them. But all girls, and if this one is a girl your pommie husband will be another one, do you get it? Now get out my truck and bring me the news as soon as you can about what sex it is.' He pushed Sarah out of the truck and slammed the door.

'But that is going to be at least sixteen weeks. It will be obvious that I am pregnant by then. What will I say to Matt?'

'Tell him you're pregnant. He doesn't need to know more than that does he?' Venter put a cigarette in his mouth and lit it.

'But we haven't had sex for ages,' she protested.

'Well, it looks like tonight is going to be his big night doesn't it.' With that Venter started his truck and drove off.

***

'Hello, Biltong. Biltong, where are you? Pick up man.'

Eventually Biltong picked up the phone.

'Biltong, what the hell is going on? We've been at the shaft nearly an hour already, why are you slinging?'

'Oh, sorry Matt. There was an emergency at twenty-two level and they needed some rails quick to build a barrier to hold back a mud slide on one of the ore passes. I am coming for you now.'

He gave three rings to indicate that man riding could commence.

***

Sarah had arrived home and, seeing a monster of selfishness in the bathroom mirror, was filled with self-loathing. The levels of her own guilt and thoughts of what might lie ahead repulsed her so much that she vomited into the sink. Emotionally and physically she had entered a nightmare scenario from which she was desperate to wake up but knew she would not. Her feelings of guilt grew deeper as she considered how her flirtatious act of a quick drink with the ever-helpful Koos Venter to spite her hard-working husband, had backfired beyond her worst possible imaginings. She thought briefly about her attention-seeking attempts at taking her life some years before, when things had not gone her own way, but quickly dumped that option as not really having the stomach for it. What was she to do? She agonised as she heard Matt's car pull into the drive.

'Hi, I'm starving,' said Matt as he walked through the door. 'What have we got for dinner?'

The decision made, Sarah pulled down her skirt revealing her favourite bright red, g-string panties and unbuttoned her blouse so her breasts peeped out of cups that could barely hold them, 'Me!'

Matt had not received such an invitation in a while and noticed immediately that Sarah had gained a little weight, 'Oh, nice surprise, but I really am starving. Can we just eat something first?'

'Another ten minutes is not going to make any difference. I have been fantasising about you all day.' Sarah pulled Matt towards her by his crotch, he capitulated quickly and tried to make a move towards the drawer for a condom. 'Oh leave that,' she said, pulling him down on top of her. 'I want to feel the real man. We are fine at this time of the month, trust me,' and seductively stuck her tongue in his mouth.

***

'Good morning, Meneer,' Matt said as he passed Symington and Coetzee and walked across the yard to the shaft area to wait for the early cage. Neither responded. He looked at his watch, it was five thirty-five. Symington and Coetzee finished their conversation and walked towards the mine offices, Symington struggling to keep up with Coetzee's gigantic strides.

As they disappeared around the corner, Biltong passed Matt an envelope with his name on it as he said good morning. It just said Davis, no Mr or Matt, just Davis. It contained a handwritten note from Symington saying,

'Come to my office before you go underground today and don't keep me waiting. The Meneer'.

Matt made his way across the yard and knocked on Symington's door. It opened and Venter was standing to the left hand side.

'Davis. Come in, come, don't hang about out there like a spineless kaffir,' said Symington.

Matt walked in and stood just off the smart rug in front of Symington's desk — he'd been warned in no uncertain terms by other miners about encroaching on Symington's mother's rug, prized as the only thing they'd managed to bring out of Rhodesia when they fled.

'Yes Meneer?'

'How would you like to start earning some real money?' asked Symington.

'Doing what, Meneer?'

'Sewing party frocks for pretty little kaffir girls to wear in the shabean whorehouse! Mining, man, gold mining! That is what we do here Davis, you imbecile, not that you pommies know much about mining, whingeing, whining limey bastards that you are.'

Venter coughed, which brought Symington's developing rant to an abrupt end.

'Ignore me, I jest. No, we need a good man that can do a special task for us, a man that wants to earn good money and a man that can keep what he sees to himself. A man that knows how to mind his own business and follows orders. Are you that kind of man, Davis?'

'Err, yes, I think so, Meneer.'

'Well, either you are or you are not Davis. Double-minded pommies.'

Venter coughed again before Symington could go off on another rant.

'Yes, I am Meneer,' Matt answered positively, the sound of crushing silk filled his ears. He'd been on the mine for six months and had earned a quarter of what he'd been earning in the UK coalfields and he was now desperate to get some money coming in.

'How much have you been earning, Davis?' asked Symington.

'On average about fifteen hundred rand a month, Meneer.'

'Well, that is not enough to keep a family of meerkats alive, is it Venter?' Symington asked his side kick with a smile.

'No. Not enough to keep a man's wife in red panties and push-up bras.' Matt didn't quite connect the dots of Venter's remarks, but that was nothing new.

'Okay then. Davis, we have a job prospecting in a remote part of the mine. It will be a small team of workers and you will need to blast at least twice a day to get to the area in time.'

'In time for what? The law says we can only blast once a day unless special ventilation facilities are provided.'

'There you go, arguing the orders already. I thought you said that you were the man?'

Matt shut up, hoping the job offer would not be retracted.

'Do you think that we would put men into a situation without the right facilities being in place?'

Matt still stood silently.

'Well do you?'

'No, of course not Meneer. I'm sorry, it was a stupid remark.'

'Yes. Stupid remark Davis. You only need to go into the tunnel and mark off the round for drilling in the morning and give the orders out for the rails, pipes and drains to be laid. You then get out of there and let the kaffirs get on with it. You blast when the round is drilled and charged with explosives and then send the kaffirs back in to clear it out for the next round.'

'But, don't I need to be there to supervise them and look out for their safety, Meneer?'

'Yes, yes, of course you do, but it is a dangerous area and the rock has many faults. You do not want to be in there should there be an earthquake do you?'

'Well no, Meneer.'

'Then let the kaffirs do what they are paid to do and you do what I am paying you to do. Does three thousand rand a month seem fair to you as basic, with another two thousand a month if you give me fifty metres advance.'

'Five thousand rand? Yes Meneer, of course I will do it. I will do it for you, Meneer,' Matt was excited; the sound of crushing silk filled his ears again.

'Yes, I am sure you will,' Symington said wryly. 'But remember, you say nothing to no one. If the word gets out that this mine is in financial trouble the kaffirs will start to riot and we will have big trouble on our hands and it will be all your fault.'

'No. I won't say anything to anyone Meneer, I promise,' Matt was emphatic.

'Including that little wife of yours,' Venter added. 'As everybody knows, pommie women can hardly keep their pants on, never mind a secret.' He winked at Symington who just raised his eyebrows.

'Right, we start next Monday. Make sure you have Joseph as your team leader and some good machine boys. You can have three of my Boys' Brigade, the Basotho are the best machine operators as they are completely mindless animals.'

'Okay Meneer, thank you.'

'Yes, yes, alright, alright, get out, get out,' said Symington impatiently, so Matt left the office.

'Do you think he will keep his mouth shut when these kaffirs find out we are going for the Black Reef and start kicking off?' asked Venter.

'By the time they actually find out where we are and what we are doing it will be too late and that pommie bastard will be the first one they will go for. We will plead ignorance and pretend we are just as outraged as they are that greed made him encroach on their Nunakulu's finger.'

'Good plan, Meneer, good plan. Blame the pommie.'

'Yes, yes. You get out as well as your big pay day won't come if you mess this one up Venter. And send that Sela in, I want some tea.'

Chapter 11

'Sarah, Sarah. You won't believe it,' Matt said excitedly as he came through the front door. 'Sarah! Where are you?'

He went through the lounge to the bedroom. Sarah was tucked up in bed and although the light brown curtains were closed the bright African sun shone through them and filled the room with light.

'Sarah. Sarah, what's wrong?' He touched her hair as she lay sleeping.

She woke and turned to him, 'I'm ill.'

'With what? Anyway, I have some great news.'

'News about what?' she asked sleepily.

'Meneer Symington has offered me a special contract, but I'm not supposed to talk about it,' quickly curbing his speech in memory of the conversation with Symington and his promise he would tell no one. 'Anyway, it is just a new contract and I am going to be getting five thousand rand a month if I hit my metres target.' The excitement grew with the realisation of the amount of money he would be earning. 'That's made you feel better already, hasn't it?'

Sarah got out of bed immediately and put on her house clothes. 'I have some great news of my own,' she put her arms around his neck and looked him straight in the eye. The opportunity to well and truly saddle Matt with the situation had so graciously presented itself. She was hoping that Matt's simple, soft underlying nature would adopt the news warmly, if she could only deliver it in the right way. With a soft smile she began.

'Things have been a bit strained between us since we have been here and I know that I have been a bit out of order sometimes with buying all the clothes and things when we didn't have money. But I was just unhappy and you were working long hours and I was bored. And I know that you have been under a lot of stress trying to earn money for us, and I really do appreciate that.' She took him by the hands and led him towards the bed to sit down. 'I have noticed you reading that Gideon's Bible you stole from the hotel room we stayed in when we first arrived. You've been leaving it on the dining table when you go out to work in the morning.'

'Well, yes, but I don't think taking a Bible is stealing they put them there for you I think. Anyway, I don't know why I took it, I just like some of the stories in the second part of the book, the first is a bit hard to understand, it's all about the Jews I think, but I only read it because of the stories. I remember when I was at Sunday school when I was very young they told us the same stories. Why? Does someone know I took it?' He started to sound worried.

'No, of course not. But your prayers have been answered.'

'What prayers? I have not been saying any prayers. I am not even sure I believe it anyway, I just like the stories. What do you mean my prayers have been answered?' Matt was astonished and looked inquisitively into Sarah's eyes.

'Well, think about it. You have been given this new contract and on the same day that I think that I am pregnant. It all makes sense and your prayers have been answered.'

'But I have not said any prayers,' he insisted.

'Well, maybe not with your mouth but maybe in your heart. You do want us to be happy don't you?' she looked directly at him, keeping her eyes as soft as possible.

It was making absolutely no sense to Matt. He sat, silent and deeply perplexed, shocked at Sarah's explanation of apparently inconsistent events. Sarah just smiled sweetly and touched her tummy in a show of motherly tenderness.

'We will be fine now. I was worried about the money and that but now I can see everything is going to be alright,' Sarah concluded.

'Alright? I can't work it out. We only made love last night, and we hadn't had any sex for . . . well, I can't remember. I have been so busy and tired from work. How can you be pregnant?'

'We women just know these things when they happen. Come on, you must be starving. Let's go and do some food and we can talk about everything over a nice dinner.' She kept hold of Matt's hand and led him slowly, like a mother does her infant child. 'It's been a while since I cooked for you, I have been so busy with the ladies book club and everything. You sit down and leave it to me.'

That night Matt felt like he had a dream. A sound like something running backwards and forwards in the loft woke him, but then it continued as he lay in bed looking directly above him at where the noise was coming from. He thought of the strange things that had been happening of late in the house. Things that in isolation seemed to have no importance. Only a week ago he and Sarah had had a usual late night argument. The night was very hot and he had got out of bed and gone into the kitchen to get his thoughts together and take a drink of water. He'd hoped it would give Sarah an opportunity to calm down. No one ever won an argument with Sarah, as Matt had learnt. There was no black and white with Sarah, only shades of grey. He remembered standing at the sink, drinking water, when there were three loud, sudden bangs, like doors being slammed very hard, so hard that the house shook. Matt went straight into the bedroom to tell Sarah to stop slamming doors and waking up the neighbourhood. She had just looked at him from the bed and replied before turning over, 'You're the one slamming doors, you idiot.' Matt realised that the doors had been slammed so fast although there were not three doors in the house close enough together to slam in such quick succession. A cold chill ran down his spine and he quickly returned to bed and pulled the quilt over his head.

So, what was the noise? He looked up at the ceiling, his heart rate rose, his mind went back to the conversation with Dirk Grayling about things that go more than bump in the night. About a spiritual world that is apparently all around us and, even more worryingly, is active all the time according to Dirk. Africa was truly a strange place for a Westerner who had come no closer to another world than through old Hammer Horror films he'd watched with his siblings on Friday nights with his face securely behind a cushion to ensure he never actually viewed the scary bits.

Why was this happening and, more importantly, where would it lead? This was the enigma that kept Matt awake for most of the night. The noise had stopped the moment he heard the sound of crushing silk, which brought a sense of calm as well as unease because he did not know why he kept hearing that sound.

***

It was the first day of the contract. Matt and Joseph, his team leader, were counting the jack hammer drilling machines and drills as they were put into mine cars and pushed towards the lift for sending down to sixteen level. The newly-assembled team seemed very much at odds with one another, the Zulu hating the Basotho and the Basotho hating everyone and everything.

The team, twenty-two in total, contained machine operators, pipe and rail fitters, winch drivers, two locomotive drivers and a team leader for each specific job with Joseph as overall team leader. The truth was that there was no real need for a white miner. The blacks knew the job better than any white European, but it was apartheid South Africa and blacks were classified as mere labourers while mine law demanded the presence of a white supervisor at all mining operations.

There was little conversation other than about getting air and water supplies to the area quickly so that they could take their first round down into the footwall of the cross cut where the Black Reef seemed to outcrop. Matt studied the survey plan that Berriman had drawn up reluctantly. It showed a winze driven into the floor of the tunnel at about forty-five degrees, about one and a half metres high and one and a half metres wide, to a depth of a hundred metres. It seemed a huge fault plane had thrust the Carbon Leader ore body downwards to an unknown depth. All Berriman's surveying on the level below had shown nothing, causing him to believe that another fault further down may have thrown the ore body in another direction.

The decision had been made for two teams to drill and blast simultaneously; one on the winze on sixteen level and another to blast a tunnel that would intersect the reef or the fault plane on eighteen level and then turn and rise up to meet the winze coming down the fault plane. This would shorten the time for exposing the reef, should it even be there. A point that Berriman still argued, under his breath if Symington was about. Meneer Coetzee was to know nothing of the additional mining for at least a month from the first blast, since it was definitely outside the mine boundary.

Coetzee was well looked after by new groups of young black girls brought in by Symington's Boys' Brigade. As Coetzee indulged his passion for the black, silky flesh of the young and vulnerable, he would, in contrast, take out his anger and self-loathing on the young black men he employed as house servants, often meting out beatings for minor offences.

In a world of addiction, whatever form it takes, the addiction of one often means dire consequences for the many and the only winner is death. One victim was Symington's pikanin, Sela. Some time after his profuse apologies following his instinctive outburst underground because of his fear that the mine was going to damage his spiritual ancestry, he was found hanging, his body burnt beyond recognition. Apparently, he had administered judgement on himself for being unable to protect his beloved and pure sister from Coetzee's lust.

Sela's sister had arrived at the mine with a security pass authorised by Symington. She had been led, unwittingly, to Coetzee's quarters in expectation of meeting her brother. After her abuse she was strangled into silence by the Boys' Brigade who then dumped her naked body outside the mine perimeter fence. Sela wrote a note to their father, found in his room at the compound, saying that he could not face the guilt of being a Shona warrior unable to defend his own flesh and blood but that what he was powerless to prevent in his physical life he would somehow avenge in the spiritual.

Chapter 12

'Are all the machines drilling?' asked Matt.

'Yes Baas,' said Joseph. 'All drilling and we will get the second round on the winze as long as we maintain air and water all shift.'

'Good man. You and I will get our bonus, Joseph.'

'I don't get bonus, Baas.'

'What, none at all?'

'No Baas, only white miners get bonus. The machine operators get a bit more the more holes they drill and we just get the same.'

'So, how much do you get paid as a senior team leader?'

'I take home five hundred rand, Baas.'

'How do you live on that? I couldn't live on fifteen hundred.'

'Baas, the reality is you work to exist here. There are no social handouts, you work or you starve, that is simply it. As a man, a proud African man, I cannot let my family starve. So I do what I have to do. May I ask you a question, Baas?'

'Yes, as long as you don't want a bite of this sandwich because I'm starving.'

Matt pulled out a jam and peanut butter sandwich from his bag, it was an improvement on what Sarah had previously made for him. She had been more accommodating since that news about the impending offspring.

'We don't understand, Baas, why do the Afrikaner treat you so badly? As a white man, I mean. I am not sure that they like you any more than they like the blacks.'

Matt held back from biting the sandwich, 'I'm not really sure. Is it that obvious?'

'Yes Baas, very much so. They even refer to you in front of the men as a white kaffir.'

Matt's head drooped as he allowed himself to think how lonely he was, it felt as though he did not have a friend in the world. He let the self-pity invade for a few moments then felt Joseph's eyes on the back of his head and looked at the excuse for a sandwich in his hand. Nothing was like he expected it to be in this gold mining adventure, the grass was no greener. As his teeth clamped around the sandwich there was a terrific bang.

The ground seemed to drop away beneath them; the sidewalls of the tunnel began to shudder and quake; the tension ropes designed to hold back rock in a seismic event began twanging like guitar strings under immense pressure; the roof dumped rock fragments all around them. Matt closed his eyes during the few seconds of the bump, as miners call it, although the episode seemed much longer.

Opening one eye he peered through the dust to see Joseph hanging onto the water pipe that ran down the sidewall.

'That was a big one, Baas,' said Joseph, standing upright and brushing the dust off his overalls.

Matt's teeth were caked in peanut butter and jam as the adrenaline pumped through his body, 'What the hell?'

'That was not good Baas. Some brothers have lost their lives here today,' Joseph lowered his head.

'You don't know that. It could have been in an old area miles away from where people are working.'

'I know what I know Baas, and my instinct is never wrong.'

First aid teams and the mine doctor passed through Matt's working place within twenty-five minutes on their way to A16 stope face. Rescue teams and digging teams followed quickly behind. The doctor was heard telling his assistants that the bump was six point five on the Richter scale.

The large figure of Dirk Grayling appeared out of the darkness. He was perspiring heavily having run from another stope some two kilometres away.

'Can I do anything to help?' asked Matt.

'Yes, follow me. We need all the men we can get.'

'Come on Joseph,' Matt said as he followed Dirk down the tunnel.

At the stope face the roof and floor of the bottom section had come together under the terrific pressure for barely a split second before relaxing and leaving a fifty centimetre gap, just enough to shine the beam of a cap lamp into. Matt shone his light into the space and saw heads and bodies crushed beyond recognition. The pressure had forced out the victims' eyes and the scene resembled a gory horror movie, which delayed the impact of what he was looking at on Matt's minds and emotions.

'Matt, Matt,' shouted Dirk. 'Get a locomotive jack from the cross cut and try and lift that corner of the roof up to see if anyone is alive under here.'

'I'm here, I'm here,' screamed the voice of Franz Joubert, a white miner. Dirk swung his light around to where the screams were coming from. Joubert's face peered back, whitewashed with dust and pupils dilated by fear.

'Get me out, get me out,' he screamed, looking down at his waist. Dirk's light followed Joubert's gaze, he was trapped by the legs and there was a huge amount of blood. It was not blood from his wounds, broken bones and minor cuts, but from where Joubert had used his own knife to try and cut away his thigh in order to release himself, causing more damage than the segment of roof that had trapped him.

'Get me out of here. The aftershock, the aftershock,' he wailed in terror, stabbing at his thigh with the knife. Dirk made his way over and tried to prevent Joubert from injuring himself more with the knife, a struggle ensued. Matt felt a new fear.

'Help me,' cried Dirk, 'Matt, help me, take this knife from him.'

Matt went over and held Joubert's arm as Dirk unwrapped his fingers one by one from the vice-like grip he had on the knife. Matt had never seen fear like that in a man's eyes before.

Joubert screamed again and again, 'Get me out. The aftershock, the aftershock.'

It was at that point Matt realised what Joubert was saying; there is always an aftershock at some point after a major seismic event, and the odds are that if the first one didn't get you, the second most likely would.

Fear rose in Matt's heart and made him feel nauseous as he grappled with the situation. They were eighteen hundred metres down and looking a second seismic event in the face. He felt panic-stricken, 'Dirk, what shall I do? What shall I do?'

'Get that loco jack as quick as you can and get back here while I try and calm him down.'

'But what about the aftershock?' questioned Matt, hoping that Dirk would just give him leave to get out of there.

Dirk took a hold of Matt by the lapel of his overalls, looked into his eyes and said, 'Did you find that faith in God I spoke to you about?'

'No!' Fear gripped his throat.

'Well, now would be a good time to start. We are in this together. You are the only one who is near enough to help me. Now go and get that jack and start praying that we can free him before the aftershock hits. For all our sakes.'

Matt ran out of the stope into the cross cut, his heart pounding so hard against the wall of his chest it felt like it might burst out any second. He ran towards the locomotive and began yanking the jack from its brackets. He yanked and yanked but it was stuck fast. He tried kicking it. Fear loomed over his head like a cloud, oppressing him. He just wanted to run away. He considered it. Why should he risk his life? Why should he? He argued with his conscience. They hate me anyway. They say I'm a white kaffir. The argument was gaining credibility in his mind as he continued to kick at the jack. Joseph came up behind him and calmly released the pin that held the jack in place. He could see that Matt was shaking and that fear was both quickening and slurring his speech.

'Baas,' he said calmly, looking into Matt's bulging and gaping eyes, 'don't be afraid. This is not your hour nor your time. You have a destiny that you will fulfil, but it is not yet.' He placed his hand on Matt's shoulder, something that in any other situation a black man would not do to a white.

Matt heard the sound of crushing silk filling his ears, filtering quickly down to his heart and calming his mind. He stopped shaking, looked at Joseph and started to apologise.

'Baas,' Joseph interrupted, 'do not apologise for being human. If a man cannot conquer his fear of death then he will be a prisoner for his entire life. You cannot control the day or the hour that you will leave this world, so why fear something over which you do not have control? If you must fear anything then fear God. For that is the beginning of wisdom.'

Matt nodded and Joseph continued, 'Go to the first aid station at the shaft and bring as many stretchers as these men can carry.'

Joseph turned to acknowledge the four men who had come up behind him. They too looked at Matt with empathy as it was obvious that the situation had got the better of him. Matt considered their acceptance of his failure in this regard and his respect for his black colleagues increased dramatically. He finally realised that they were in this together; death was going to show no favours to race or creed.

This was the hour for a man to be a man he pondered. An hour to face his weakness and his natural fear of death. He asked himself: can I harness the power of this fear for good? Can I make this power of fear serve my need in this hour? Can I make fear my friend and wring out of it the opposite reaction? These were wise considerations for a man who, only moments earlier, was as a mouse caught in a trap, fear robbing him of his physical and mental powers to the point that he could neither think logically nor take the simplest of actions. All things were now calm in his mind. Had Joseph cast some kind of spell on him? The reversal of his mind state had been almost instant. As Matt walked down the tunnel towards the shaft, the four men following, a new and heightened sense of his own self became evident.

It is not the absence of fear that makes men courageous, he concluded, but the acceptance that fear is part of the make up of human kind. What could a man really achieve if he should see fear as a positive gift, the twin brother of courage? The one twin is no less or no more than the other. They have the same father, because both fear and courage are produced in the heart of a man. Why is one considered good and one bad? The question lingered.

Where did this heightened sense of understanding come from so instantaneously? Matt felt like a new creation. Many things seemed to come into focus, not least that he did indeed have a destiny to fulfil, if he could only fathom what it actually was.

Six hours later the death toll was forty-seven dead, sixty-seven stretchered out of the mine and a boy had become a man.

Chapter 13

'How many metres are we down the winze, Matt?' asked Symington.

Matt was surprised that the Meneer had used his first name, usually it was Davis this, Davis that, 'Oh, we are a hundred and thirty-seven metres down.'

'That is a good pommie. I like your advances, good advances. And how about the tunnel? How far are we away from the cross cut position?'

'Not as good. We had two days of misfires and eventually I had to light the round with a match as we couldn't find a break in the electric circuit that was causing the problem.'

'You stupid pommie bastard, don't you know that these kaffirs will try anything to sabotage the job? Think about all the money you have lost in those two rounds.'

'I did Meneer, I did. It has cost me three hundred rand.'

'No, it has cost you six hundred, because I am taking another three hundred off your contract for being a half wit lazy bastard. Koos!' shouted Symington.

'Yes Meneer,' Venter's head popped round the corner like a rabbit out of hat. He had actually been outside, listening to the whole conversation at the behest of Symington and knew all along the advances that had been made.

'Koos, take three hundred rand off Davis's contract and see to it that he uses slow burners to ignite the face so that we don't get any more misfires.'

Matt's heart sank. He and Joseph had worked all out to get another round off on Sunday morning to catch up a little.

'Get out of my sight Davis and get that job working properly.'

Matt turned around and went out of the office and across the yard towards the shaft. Once he was out of earshot Symington and Venter burst into laughter.

'He is a dumb pommie. He does not even know that we plan in several misfires per month on any contract, but that will make him work harder to recover his lost money.'

Venter's laughter grew louder at the thought, higher than Symington's until Symington stopped abruptly and said, 'Okay Venter. You have no room to talk. You can't take a piss without getting some women pregnant.'

'Oh Meneer,' he whined, 'you know I just want a son to carry on my good name.'

'A good name! Any son of yours will have a dick like a thoroughbred horse and pig shit for brains but a good name he will never have. Now get out and get yourself down the mine and make sure that pommie get his rounds off.'

Venter left the office liked a whipped dog. Once outside he saw his pikanin coming across the yard and called him over then began beating him around the head and in his face, blow after blow until eventually he fell to the ground. Venter kicked him in the small of his back and said, 'Get my bag ready to go underground, kaffir.'

Biltong watched the event from his cabin and thought, 'One day, just one day Venter we will see who will be the kaffir on that day, hey?'

***

'So, it is a boy then?' Sarah rang the Doctor's surgery for confirmation.

'Pretty sure,' replied the nurse. 'Twenty-four weeks.'

'Oh, thank God. He will be so excited,' she felt such relief as her thoughts turned towards a new life as the eventual wife of the manly Koos, since she was the only one to give him a son.

Although they had had several secret meetings since the day she had found out she was pregnant, there had been no further relationship between them. Koos, mindful of her delicate position, did not want anything to create a problem with the pregnancy and had given strict instructions to Sarah that her dim husband was not to have any sex with her either. Venter himself, on the other hand, was relentless in his carousing and had been caught recently with the young wife of a learner official. He denied it of course when Sarah heard about it. His tearful apology, saying that he had got hopelessly drunk and that the woman had come on to him in his weakened state, placated Sarah, mindful as she was of similar misdemeanours in her own life.

Sarah put down the telephone and began to dream about the wonderful life that lay ahead of her. The changes that it would bring, not only into her life but to the life of Koos, as he would now settle down into a proper relationship having found the thing he wanted most in the world, a son. And she was the one who had given it to him, a sublime utopia was on the horizon she concluded.

Chapter 14

'Why are these men not drilling?' asked Matt.

'They have heard that we are getting close to the mine boundary and that we are after Nunakulu's finger,' replied Joseph.

'Who has told them that?' he demanded.

'One of the Basotho drillers was drunk in the shabean last night and started telling the Shona tribesmen that he and his team were going take their inheritance, and then their lives, and then their women and children. That is because, once the Basotho had taken Nunakulu's finger they would be powerless to stop them. Well, a fight broke out and four were killed, seven received stab and slash wounds. The mine security broke it up with salt cartridges from shotguns and tear gas.'

Some months before those words would have made Matt recoil in disbelief, but not anymore. Other events had hardened his emotions to such barbarity, on the basis that they were almost a daily occurrence.

'So why are we not drilling?' he demanded again.

'Three of those who died were your drill operators and these others are in fear of their lives if what they have heard is true. Is it true Baas?' Joseph looked into Matt's eyes.

Matt said nothing, just looked back at him, 'Do you believe this nonsense about Nunakulu's finger? You, a God-fearing Zulu warrior?'

'Of course no, Baas. But I am a Zulu and this is not our inheritance. If I were a Shona, it would not be about the gold, it is about spiritual heritance, an identification of a special place and time, like the white man's Jerusalem.'

'You see what I mean about religion? It makes men crazy.'

'Are they any more crazy than those whose god is gold?' asked Joseph. 'Men die here one way or another. Do you think that the men who give their lives in the pursuit of gold and a day's wage will not give their lives to defend their honour and spiritual heritage? If we are going after their heritage then I can assure you of this, no one who touches it will ever see the light of day again. I had a vision last night Baas, and I tell you this, it will be the end of us all.'

The sound of crushing silk filled Matt's ears. He was angry. He was so close to earning some good money at last, so close to getting his life in order, his wife only had three months left to the birth of their child, the tunnel and winze had only forty metres to intersection, now this bad juju bullshit was getting in the way.

'Joseph, do the other tribes feel the same way as you?'

'Only the Basotho will work here Baas. They have no feelings or sympathy for the Shona, they hate them with a vengeance.'

'Then,' Matt replied, 'we will get more Basothos and finish this job and you and I will get paid. If I give you a thousand rand of my bonus will you help me finish this job Joseph? That's two month's money to you.'

Joseph took a step back and looked intently at Matt, 'I am Joseph Tetu, son of Tetu Umlayne a Zulu Chief and tribal leader of the Province of Eshetu. You would buy me like a chicken in a market? But of course, I am a poor man. No, a poor black man. Do you think you can insult my integrity for two month's pay?'

'I can see that I have offended you Joseph. I did not mean to, I thought it may help. I was wrong and I can understand what you mean. I have learnt many things in the months that I have been here. I have seen things that I wished I had never seen. Things that have taken me to the very edge of a rational mind. Things I cannot explain as a simple man from England. I had never even so much as heard about such things before and if I had heard about them I would have thought that they were just made up stories about things that go bump in the night.'

'Tell me Baas, tell me what you have seen and heard.'

'Wait a minute,' said Matt and shouted, 'pikanin.'

His pikanin came running and knelt before him.

'What have I said about kneeling in front of me?' Matt snapped. 'Anyway, go to the Meneer Symington and tell him we have a problem with the machine operators and they refuse to drill. Ask him to send me six more Basothos. Hurry.'

'Baas, you must not stop the men kneeling in front of you. They are not kneeling to you as a white man but as a chief, a superior. It is their culture and they will respect you less if you take away their dignity and freedom to show you respect. These men have already given you a new name on the mine.'

'Yes, I know, Mulungu, white shit.'

'No Baas, that was only in the beginning,' Joseph started laughing.

'Yes, very funny Joseph, you keep laughing. I have had crap from everyone since I have been here.'

Joseph stopped his laughter, 'No, not anymore Baas. They now call you Madoda, a good man. They know that you do not hate them because they are black; you are the first white man to win their hearts and minds on this mine.'

Matt's heart warmed at that news.

Joseph continued, 'All the threats, the violence and the intimidation that the Afrikaners have delivered over many years has only hardened our resolve to one day be free and that day is coming. Baas, you have showed them in the short period that you have been here that white men do have hearts and compassion, when they have not been poisoned with the sickness of apartheid and white man's delusion of being a superior race. Look at how quickly the tunnels have advanced since you took the contract. The bosses upstairs will not tell you that you have broken every mine record with your tunnel advances.'

Matt, with a look of disbelief on his face, replied, 'Have I? We? You, me and the team? Hang on though, the Meneer has just taken six hundred rand off me for the misfires, the bastard.'

Joseph just raised his eyebrows.

'Do you know what Joseph? When this tunnel is finished and we have struck the reef I am going to take my money and go and get a job on another mine. Will you come with me Joseph?'

Joseph looked directly at Matt and in a hollow tone said, 'Some people come into our lives for only a moment in time Baas, for a reason and a purpose. We will journey on together, of that I am sure, but not at this mine or any other.'

He changed the subject, 'Baas, you were going to tell me about what you had seen and heard.'

'Okay, whilst we are waiting for my pikanin to come back from the Meneer. Is the winze drilling?'

'Yes Baas. They are Basothos there, they could not wait to get at it this morning after last night's carnage.'

Matt began, 'This is going to sound really weird but remember when we first started to work together and I was getting terrible headaches all the time?'

Joseph's thoughts went to a much deeper place than the one Matt was asking him to recall. He nodded, 'Yes Baas. That was from the nitroglycerine in the explosive. Everybody gets that when they first start using it, until you build up to a level in your bloodstream.'

'I know, but I never seemed to build a tolerance to it. Then one night I took my wife out to see her new friend Irene at the town of the sister mine at Krugarsburg. It was a very warm night and I wanted to walk to clear my thoughts.'

Matt thought fleetingly about the friend that Sarah had found, seemingly from nowhere. It now struck him as quite odd as he recalled it post the event. Irene was, in fact, another of Venter's notches on the bed post and she had contacted Sarah wanting to dish as much dirt as possible about how Venter had abandoned her not six months previously, after their second girl was born.

'Well, I left my wife at the house and went for a walk and wandered past this old barn where these people were having a church meeting or something. Only there were drums and guitars. It sounded more like a party and the thing that struck me was that the whites and the blacks were all together.'

'I know the one you mean,' Joseph acknowledged.

'Well, anyway, I didn't know how long Sarah was going to be so I thought I will go in and have a look. It was either that or go to a bar and that would only mean having some trouble with the local Afrikaners.'

On going into his local bar for a drink Matt had had several encounters with Afrikaners that had ended in a hasty retreat to the sound of gunfire. Most Afrikaners had a licence to possess firearms – not a privilege extended to blacks under apartheid – so many a drunken brawl would end in a firefight of some sort.

'I sat right at the back,' Matt continued, 'and just watched as they sang a couple of songs and all danced and clapped. It was like the miner's welfare on a Friday night, only there was no beer.'

'What is the miner's welfare?' Joseph asked.

'Never mind. Anyway, a man at the front motioned for the band to stop playing and then he said something that made me very anxious, like there was some big hand over my head pointing at me.'

'What did he say Baas?' Joseph seemed transfixed, hanging on Matt's every word.

'He said, there is a man in here that is suffering from severe headaches and God wants to heal him. I thought, no it cannot be me, no one knows me here, it cannot be. I hoped against hope that he wasn't referring to me and I didn't believe in God anyway. I gripped my chair and just sat still. There was no way I was moving and eventually, after he had asked a couple of times, this young man got up and walked to the front where this man then took him and said some sort of prayer over him. I was so relieved. The band started up again and they carried on for about thirty seconds before the man motioned again for the band to stop playing. What he said next was like an arrow through my heart. He said, the man who God is talking about is still sat here. I had never felt such a conviction about anything in my life but I kind of knew without question he was referring to me. I was undone. I did not know or believe in any kind of God, but this one knew who I was and I knew, although I don't know how, that he knew everything about me.'

'And so, what did you do then?' Joseph queried.

'I found myself walking to the front. I stepped very quietly, trying to avoid making any noise. There must have been two hundred people in that barn but I don't recall seeing one of them as I walked towards this man who was smiling at me from ear to ear. Before I could say anything the man, who was a typically big South African, had put his arms around me and hugged me like a child. My heart just broke and I sobbed openly, I didn't care who was there or who was watching, I needed a friend. The days of darkness, the racist abuse and the loathing that I had endured for over eight months since arriving in this country was now being dissolved away like dirt from a window being washed away by pure clean rain.'

'I have heard good things about that place,' Joseph said. 'They are not religious people, they just have simple faith, the way it should be. So, did you experience anything?'

'This man prayed a prayer over me but I didn't really hear it. I was away in another place and a smile seemed to appear in my heart. That is the only way I can describe it. I drove home that night with Sarah rabbiting in my ears, but I cannot remember the journey. Even in the morning I felt different. The headache was gone. Does that sound crazy to you?' asked Matt.

'Crazy? This is Africa. What is crazy to outsiders is normal here. We do not try to suppress the spirit world nor do we try to pretend that it does not exist; it is all around us and is active all the time. Sometimes it crosses over and we get a glimpse, but for the most part it works in the shadows. There are those who try to use the powers for good, others for evil. Mankind is given freedom to choose his own path, but all paths must lead somewhere. A man's choices and his motives decide the path he takes but not to where it leads. That is a different set of laws beyond the control of men in this world. As the blind lead the blind and both fall into a pit.'

'You've lost me,' Matt replied.

'But that is not really what you were going to tell me, was it Baas?'

Matt and Joseph stared at one another until the silence was broken by Symington yelling, 'Davis, stop playing kaffir booty with that Zulu dog and get over here.'

Joseph smiled wryly as Matt walked past him towards Symington leaning against the tunnel sidewall who blamed his exhaustion on the beating he had given Matt's pikanin for not immediately kneeling when he entered his presence. Matt looked at his pikanin, a small Lesotho boy of about seventeen who was shaking violently and bleeding, and realised that his own lack of understanding had caused a confusion in this young lad that had led to him getting a severe beating. Inside Matt raged at himself and at Symington, outside the only evidence was a bitten lip and profuse sweating. Everything in him wanted to rip that fat pig's head off. He calmed a little and said, 'Meneer, you did not have to beat him. He is only a new boy and does not understand how things work around here.'

'Well, he has learnt pretty quick now hasn't he, Davis? Remember Davis, the only good kaffir is a dead one and until that day we just have to suffer them.'

He wiped the boy's blood and his own sweat from the silver knob of his cane. His remark was Matt's flash point.

'You fat racist pig,' he stuck his face nose to nose with Symington's. 'You're a big man aren't you? Hiding behind your position here with that cane that you wield like some half-arsed king's sceptre. Any one of these natives could take that from you and bludgeon your fat arse to death with it, you bloated sow, you excuse for a man. No, less than a man. The best part of you your mother farted out when giving birth to you.'

Symington reeled backwards and Matt believed for a millisecond that he had actually just said all that to Symington. Then he realised it was just a scene he had played out in his mind, but how he wished it was true.

The longer he worked in this place the more he despaired of himself and the, so-called superior, white race who, to his mind, were not even equal in humanity to the kaffirs they so despised and terribly abused. They were cowards to a man, intimidation, physical size and a law that meant only they had access to a loaded gun were the weapons they all hid behind. But the reality was that the blacks were true and formidable warriors and that this apartheid regime was going to blow like a seismic event one day. It will overrun them faster than the lava that covered the residents of Pompeii and I don't want to be around when it does, he thought. The sound of crushing silk filled his ears.

'Are you listening, Davis?' Symington protested. 'Where is my Black Reef you promised me?'

'I promised you?' Matt responded in surprise.

'Yes. The moment you took this contract you promised it to me by acceptance.'

Matt just sighed. This man was never wrong about anything in his own eyes, making up the policies and his own version of events on the hoof. What an evil, self-righteous twat he was. Then he said, without any conviction whatsoever, 'Yes Meneer. We have had some problems with the drill operators as they found out that we were looking for the Black Reef and refused to drill.'

'Did I not give you my Boys' Brigade? They don't give two shits about the Shona and their Nunakulu's finger.'

'I know, Meneer. But one of them died last night in the faction fighting. Another is in the hospital remember? He almost lost his leg in that roof fall we had last week. A very bad accident, he will never walk again.'

'Is he still breathing?' asked Symington.

'Is he breathing? What do you mean, is he breathing?' Matt was completely at a loss as to where Symington was taking the conversation. He turned and looked towards Joseph as if he would give him some clarity.

'If he is breathing he is still a kaffir and the only good kaffir is a dead one. Did I not tell you that Davis? At the moment he is costing me medical bills. So it would be better on my budgets if you'd let that dog bleed to death down here. Venter would have let him die. He knows what this job is all about and you'd better smarten up quickly if you are ever going to survive here. These kaffirs don't care about you, they would kill you sooner than look at you. I know all about them calling you Madoda, but you're just a white kaffir, only one rung further up the ladder of humanity than they are.'

Matt was wounded deeply by those remarks but enough was enough, 'Venter is a racist dog and you are no more than a "when we", tyrant, racist pig. I should take that cane of yours and beat your fucking head in with it and put God out of his misery having to watch the evil bastard that you are take another breath of his good air.' Matt's nose was now against Symington's and he glared, unflinching, into his eyes. Another remark from Symington would have sealed his fate in a moment. Matt was more angry than he had ever been in his life. The job, the money, neither mattered anymore. 'You fat, weasel bastard. You have crossed a line of no return,' Matt concluded.

Symington raised his cane slowly up between their faces, breathed on the silver knob and began polishing it with his handkerchief. Matt took hold of it halfway up the shaft, thinking that Symington was going to try and hit him with it.

'That is a good pommie. I knew you would get there in the end. That is the problem with you pommies, you have to be pushed so hard before you see the light. You see? Pushed hard enough and in the right direction we are all racists really. You hate me for hating the kaffirs, I hate you just for being a pommie. Your hatred of me is just another form of racism as you don't understand me or where I came from, no more than you do these kaffirs. If you had seen your father decapitated by those bastard blacks just after they had cut his balls off and shoved them into his mouth, then watched your teenage cousin raped and then bludgeoned to death with a fence post, then your six-month-old niece picked up out of her cot by the ankles and slammed against a wall with such force that her brains came out of her mouth then just dumped back into the cot, do you think that you would ever look at them as more than kaffirs? Well do you?' he raised his voice, demanding a response.

Matt lowered his eyes, he had no response

'Well do you?' demanded Symington again.

'Well, I suppose not. But you cannot blame a whole race or creed for the actions of the minority can you?'

'I don't know. Can you? Have the pommies forgiven all the Germans yet? No, let us come up to date, it was only five years ago when there were race riots in England I recall. The mid to late seventies wasn't it?'

Matt said nothing. He remembered those days well. How, as a child, he had watched and applauded some local men physically removing an Indian family who had purchased a corner shop and marching them out of the area; even the local police were complicit with such things in those days and turned a blind eye.

'You see,' Symington went on, 'racism is the best gift God gave to humanity. It is built into our genes, we are all racists. The mixing of races is a powder keg of possibilities that only requires a good spark to set it off, and that is how we work these kaffirs against each other. We don't have to teach them to butcher and maim one another. They are more than happy to do that themselves, we just give them the spark on occasion and it helps keep the numbers down.

And whilst they are busy killing one another we just keep taking the lucre, like this Nunakulu's finger, it is gold ore just like any other gold ore and it is going to make you and I very rich.'

'Make me rich? How is it going to make me rich?'

The men now stood apart and looked just like businessmen talking.

'The gold bar I have estimated to be about five hundred tons at a grade of a thousand grams per ton. At the current gold price that will make about forty million rand and, although you are a pommie, you are my pommie who is going to make us all rich and so it seems only right and fair, even though you are a pommie, that you get a cut. How does a million rand sound to you?'

'A million?' Matt could barely believe his luck; he was spending it in his mind already.

'Davis, Davis. Come back into the room,' Symington said heartily. 'You are one of my men now and I always look after my men.'

Without thinking through the connotations of that remark Matt said, 'Oh yes, Meneer, yes. One of your men, just like Venter, only not like him if you know what I mean?'

Joseph remained at a distance and said under his breath, 'No, no, no. Please no, Baas.' He walked away, muttering about the love of money being the root of all evil.

Symington shouted after him, 'Get those machines drilling or there will no food in the compound tonight, kaffir. Yes, Venter, he has been a loyal old shepherd dog for me over the years but he has become obsessed with his bloodline and has taken to impregnating every female that comes within a yard of him. He wants a son to carry on his Boer bloodline of farmers and sacky sacky dancers.'

Matt laughed at the comment at Venter's expense.

'You see,' said Symington, 'you're just as racist as me.'

Matt neither agreed nor disagreed.

'But don't laugh at Venter too much,' he said, lowering his voice momentarily, 'he has managed to get that wife of yours into more than the book club.'

Chapter 15

'Sarah, Sarah!' shouted Matt. 'Where are you?'

'I'm here in the bedroom, resting. I haven't felt very well today. Can you get your own dinner?'

Venter had left only an hour before and there had been very little resting. He'd reminded her in his own romantic manner that she was merely pregnant, not a quadruped, and therefore her hands and mouth were well capable of fulfilling his immediate needs.

'Tell me,' Matt shouted, 'tell me that that baby is mine and you've not been behind my back with Venter.'

Matt took hold of her by the shoulders, 'Look into my eyes and tell me the truth.' Although she began to deny any such thing, she had that 'I've been in the coalhouse' look that Matt knew so well. 'You fucking slut,' he cried out.

His heart broke in two and tears welled up. He walked up and down the room wanting to punch Sarah. She could see real anger in his eyes and pulled the quilt over her, raising her knees to her chest. Her guilt was real and she knew that she may as well just front up and say that their relationship was over; that in her eyes it had been over before they even came to this country; that she had found a true man in Koos Venter and now that the baby was sure to be a boy she was the woman he had always been looking for.

Matt, half-speaking, half-wailing, cried out, 'How much can one person take?'

He turned head and heart upwards as though talking to God, the sound of crushing silk filled his ears and he sank to his knees and wept uncontrollably.

'I can't take anymore,' he sobbed. 'I've had enough.'

Sarah seized the moment to make her exit and drove to the mine social club in town to find Koos and tell him of the developments. She knew he would understand and support her wholeheartedly, he loved her, she was the mother of his child. Then the magnitude of the situation struck her soul like a hammer.

***

'What are you doing here, Baas?' asked Joseph. 'This compound is for kaffirs you know.'

'Joseph, Joseph, for a moment Symington had me, but I am not one of them, no matter how he likes to put it. And I never will be. Racism is not about the colour of the skin, or anything like that, it is about choice. It is an attitude and I choose to be one who will try to choose what I know to be morally right, no matter what the situation is.'

He took the beer bottle Joseph was about to put to his lips and drank from it. The rest of the group sat around the fire went completely silent. It was an unthinkable situation in their eyes, not just that this white man came into their living quarters like he was one of them, but that he drank from the same bottle as a black man. Making space for him around the fire, they seemed honoured by his presence and quickly sent the new boy, young Thomas, to get some more beer from the shabean telling him no hanging around after the girls, they will chew you up and spit you out.

'Are you going to tell me what you really wanted to tell me that day when we spoke about the headaches and church meeting? Before Meneer Symington interrupted us,' Joseph asked.

'Not here and now, I just want to get pissed and probably fight somebody.'

'Baas, you are amongst friends. Why would you want to fight somebody?'

'It is just the way I used to deal with things when they went wrong. I would go to the welfare, get pissed, pick a fight with someone and after that shake hands and have a pint.'

Joseph looked at him as father to a wayward son.

'Baas, it does not work like that here you know that. You pick a fight with an African man and one of you is going to die. There will be no shaking of hands and having a beer. Depending which tribe you choose, you will be left with your balls stuffed down your throat or your eyeballs gouged out. That is not the way to leave this world, is it?'

Matt lowered his head in acknowledgement of the truth he knew his friend was speaking, 'No, you're right Joseph. I am only talking out of my pain and anger. Would you walk with me?'

Thomas came back with the beer. He'd only managed to purchase three beers for the ten rand that Joseph had given him, the Boys' Brigade had taken advantage.

It was winter on the high veld. The night was cool and crisp. They walked along the perimeter fence of the compound.

'Venter has done you the worst kind of wrongs Baas. If that was a black man he would die for that. A visit to the witchdoctor, followed by the curse and his days would be numbered. Or he would be necklaced at the edge of the village as a warning to others.'

'You know about it? How do you know about it?' Matt asked with a good deal of embarrassment.

'Baas, everybody knows about it. One of the shift bosses pikanins heard them talking as Venter was doing his usual bragging.'

'Why did you not tell me? Why did no one tell me?'

'Baas, you are white man. It is not the place of any of us to speak to you about such things. A woman should be the glory of her husband not his shame. In our culture they would both be taken to knife.'

'But I thought you were a Christian man?'

'I am. And although that runs deeply in my heart, as does forgiveness, and although I know if I don't forgive I will not be forgiven, my cultural traditions can be a terrible challenge to that faith. That is what being a true Christian is all about. Replacing love for hate, revenge with forgiveness. Even when that is against everything we believe to be right and true. Do you want to kill Venter?' asked Joseph.

'Of course I do. I want to cut out his black heart from his big Boer chest and feed it to his dog.'

Joseph threw his head back and laughed out loud, 'You have got Africa well and truly in your blood.'

Matt could do no more than laugh with him

'I think we should necklace him,' Joseph almost squealed with laughter at the thought and bent over double in hysterics.

'What is necklacing?' asked Matt, also bent double.

'It is putting a car tyre around his neck, tying him to a post and setting the tyre on fire.'

They both howled with laughter.

'That's evil,' said Matt.

The hysterical laugher continued, they held onto each other's arms as they carried on their discourse.

'Why are we laughing? That is not a very Christian thing to do is it?' asked Matt, still unable to control his laughter.

'No,' replied Joseph, 'and necklacing is too good for the likes of Venter.'

As the laughter reached a stage where speech was impossible, Matt just managed to say, 'That would be the best hog roast I'd ever been to.'

Both men nearly passed out with hysteria. When they had resumed a more controlled conversation Joseph said, 'He will burn Baas. In this life or the next, but Venter will burn and that is no laughing matter. He has feet that are swift to run to evil, and evil begets evil. His fate is certain and sealed by his own actions. Unless he turns and seeks true forgiveness, which is not likely in Venter's case. I think there are two kinds of men that will never find peace with God, those like Venter who cannot think their way out of a paper bag or see the truths that are in front of them, and those who are so intelligent, like Meneer Symington, their arrogance blinds them to any truth other than that of personal gain.'

There was silence for a few moments and both men just looked at the ground.

'What am I going to do?' asked Matt. 'What would you do?'

'Baas, I don't think that you have choice in this matter; the choice of the next immediate phase of your life has been taken from you. Are you going to bring up a child that is not yours? Are you going to continue with a relationship that is one-sided, with a woman who has brought such shame upon you? No, you have no choice, as I see it.'

Matt finally said, 'I knew this day would come the day we got married. I did not really want it then and I certainly don't want it now. I knew that when I stood in that church and said the vows. I thought, if there is a God he knew that I was lying.'

'You're right, Baas, and he did know, but no coward will enter the kingdom of God.'

'So, I am doomed on that front as well then?' Matt asked dejectedly.

Joseph smiled at him and replied, 'No Baas. All things for you now are forgiven, since that day you simply took Jesus as your saviour. But you have to finish your destiny.'

'What destiny? I am just a man of England from the coal fields. What is this destiny you refer to? Yes, I now believe in God and have a very simple faith, but I am not sure about any kind of destiny. Who am I that I should have any kind of destiny?'

'You were born for such a time and place as this and although this is only one small pocket of a regime of wickedness that spans the continent of Africa, a small spark will set a whole forest aflame, especially South Africa,' Joseph replied.

'Forest and flames. What the hell are you talking about?' Matt was rattled and frustrated by Joseph's incomprehensible analysis.

'The end of something is often better than its beginning,' Joseph continued, 'and the end of this situation you find yourself in will be your making and your destiny. But you must fulfil it. You were chosen from the beginning of time for this moment. Your whole life has led up to this point. Do not let cowardice now rob it from you.'

Matt had a moment of epiphany when things that were clouded in his mind became clear. Why was he here, in this godforsaken place, and what on earth possessed him to come here? It had seemed so innocent in the newspaper advert.

Joseph interrupted Matt's thoughts.

'This place is not forsaken by God and that is the point. You are the spark that God has chosen to set the forest ablaze. Now tell me about that night the enemy came to sift you.'

Matt was completely taken by surprise at that question. He looked at Joseph and asked, 'Who are you Joseph? How do you know all these things?'

'I am Joseph son of Tetu . . .'

'I know all that,' Matt interrupted. 'You told me that when you accused me of trying to buy you like a chicken in the marketplace. I mean, who are you really? You are not like any other man that I have ever met.'

'Baas, tell me please about the night that the enemy came to sift you.'

'The enemy? Why do you call him that?'

'He goes by many names which would you prefer? Satan, Lucifer, Diablo, the Devil, Son of Perdition?' Joseph responded impatiently. 'Now tell me about the night the enemy came to sift you.'

Chapter 16

'I was sat one morning about ten thirty on a Saturday that we had off.'

'Yes, I know the day and the hour.'

'How do you know?' asked Matt, 'and if you know, why are you pressing me to tell you?'

'I know that the situation occurred. I was praying for you that your foot would not slip and that you would not let fear cause you to stumble and that you would have the victory in the end. I want to hear your understanding of that situation,' Joseph stood and looked into Matt's eyes.

'Who are you?' Matt asked again, quietly.

Joseph fixed his gaze and said, 'Later. Now tell me.'

'Well, it all started one night when Sarah and I were arguing as usual and we were in bed. As I had to get up at four thirty I said that's it, I'm going to sleep in the living room, on the sofa. I went into the room. I did not put on the light but put the gas fire on as it was a bit chilly and just lay down on the sofa. I had only been there a couple of minutes when I heard someone walking around in the room. I lay with my head on the cushion, straining my eyes in the half-light, trying to make out any shapes. I could clearly see the table and chairs of the dining set, most things really, but I could not see the shape that was making the noise. As the sound came close and almost felt like it touched me I felt cold sweat start to run down my face, my heart was pounding so hard I thought I would have a cardiac arrest. I was absolutely terrified. Just at the moment that I thought I was going to die there, I heard a voice say, "don't be afraid, turn off the fire and go back to bed. Leave it for now". And immediately, just like someone had pulled the plug from a water-filled sink, the fear drained away and my heartbeat slowed dramatically, very unnatural. I had the sense of mind to get up, switch off the fire and go to bed. I must have gone immediately to sleep, which is crazy when you think of the situation, but woke for work at the usual time. My first thought was blimey, that was a strange dream, one of those that seemed too real for comfort. I got up and went into the kitchen, made myself my usual mug of tea and then went into the living room. I was horrified to see that the cushions were arranged at one end of the sofa as I had left them and the lid of the gas fire was raised where I had switched it off. My blood ran cold.

The following Saturday I was just sat reading that old paperback Bible you gave me when I felt that I heard someone say to me, "you have never blessed this house". I thought, blessed this house, what does that mean? Truly, some very scary things had happened since we came into this house, but bless the house, what did that mean? So, I went from room to room and just said in each room, "I bless this room in Jesus' name", and after I had gone through all the rooms I went to sit back down on the chair. Then the voice said, "now do it with the blood of Christ". I thought, what nonsense is that? But there was no answer, and I have to admit I felt a real idiot going through the house saying "I bless this room in the blood of Christ". I was telling myself it was crazy until I came to the kitchen. As I said the words the room turned to monochrome. Black and white like an old movie and I could see what surely looked like blood running down the walls. I shook my head until the image went and then sat down, shocked and worried.'

'Go on,' said Joseph.

'On the following Wednesday night, I was alone. Sarah had gone to the book club and it always seemed to run over late.'

Joseph merely raised his eyebrows.

'Yes well, anyway, we know all that now don't we? I was just relaxing on the couch when I became aware of a great presence of evil. The presence was thick and tangible, and I did not need to ask what it was. It was pure evil. I heard a voice speaking to me, saying, "he has come to determine whether you truly believe in what you did the other day". I then felt someone pulling at my feet and as I looked down towards the end of the couch I thought I saw Sarah playing with them. Oh, I thought, I'm only dreaming, it's Sarah. At the very second I thought that, the room was gone and I was in total darkness, a huge being picked me up, upside down by my feet and, although I could not see him, he said, "I am going to crucify you". I have to say at this point, I do not remember everything that happened over the next half hour. I believe some memories were taken from me to protect my sanity, but I will come back to that later. I remember being totally terrified and I knew that this was no dream. I didn't know what to do or to say, so I tried to struggle violently, but I had no power whatsoever over the situation. It was only when I cried out, "Jesus help me, help me", did the room seem to come back and I was being gently laid back down on the couch. Then someone or something was doing things with my legs that are not possible, literally tying them in knots. I know it sounds crazy but that is what I remember."

Matt took a long breath, seemingly still frightened by the event, then he continued.

'I then remember knowing that I had to get up and fight and that I did have authority in this situation. Only I did not know how or why I had it, I just knew I had it, and that the only thing that was going to overpower me was what I allowed to. I remember then engaging in almost a physical fight with something whose face I never saw. I really don't remember much about that, only that I won in some way. My enemy then changed his tactics and sat cross-legged in front of me. There was no room this time, everything was white. Not brilliant white, just empty and there was no floor, no walls or ceiling, although we sat. He was a very attractive looking man with the darkest eyes and olive skin; he seemed to be wearing a white knitted sweater, not unlike a fisherman's sweater. He said nothing. Just stared into my eyes. He never blinked and then I heard the sound of a baby crying. It was as if I knew that it was the crying of my, as yet unborn, baby. The man in front of me remained silent, but with his eyes he caused me to look to my left where there was a bundle wrapped in a black cloth, suggesting that this was a baby. Then he spoke, saying, "she belongs to me". I looked and leant towards the bundle, and replied, "no, she belongs to the Lord Jesus Christ", and I drew my hand across the bundle in the sign of the cross. Are you still with me, Joseph?'

Joseph just nodded, like he knew exactly what Matt was talking about.

'Are you not shocked?'

Joseph smiled wryly and just said, 'Carry on.'

'Well, it all goes a big vague after that. The last thing I remember was that I knew the fight was over and I was back in the room, but not back in my body. I could see myself laying on the couch like I was fast asleep, and I knew that I had to get back into my body. This is the real crazy bit of it all for me. I could see my head and face out the corner of my eyes as I lay down on top of myself and just as my head seemed to click into my head, I woke. I sat up and then immediately fear, like a wave in a roaring ocean, started to rush up over me. I started to shake uncontrollably, my heart was pounding and pounding and I thought again I was going die of heart failure. Then I felt a hand placed on my head, just above my scalp into my hair, and it felt that I was forgetting some of the things that had just happened, like they were being taken from me.

My heart rate slowed and the fear became manageable. The next moment Sarah came home, making her usual excuse for being late, but I just brushed past her and went into town. I needed a drink and time to gather my thoughts. Do you think I am going crazy?'

'No, the house where you live has a history and the shift boss who lived there before you was only there two weeks before he was found hanging in the garage. The house itself has no relevance to the activity really; it is the ground on which it stands. Before apartheid and the arrival of the whites that place was the home of the Sangoma Theatsu. He was a very powerful witch doctor who liked to . . . work the very dark side of his craft. The whites resettled his family into the township. When I say resettled, of course I mean herded like Jews to the concentration camps. They are still no more than squatter camps to this day. Theatsu cursed the ground and any who live on it. Ever since that day that place has driven men and their families to horrible murders and suicides.'

Matt could hardly believe what Joseph had just divulged.

'Why did they give me that house?' Matt asked angrily.

'It was at Venter's request that you got that house and Meneer Symington wholeheartedly agreed. They've wanted to destroy you since you got here.'

'But why?' Matt asked dejectedly, 'I only came to work and wanted to work hard.'

Joseph put his hand on Matt's shoulder and said, 'Apartheid is more than skin deep, you know that now too well yourself. And yet they were themselves being used. They are like many men who believe that they control their own destiny and they think that their decisions are always their own choices. How wonderfully well the enemies of all mankind manipulate men's hearts into arrogance that is beyond arrogance; the spiritual forces of darkness who sit manipulating humanity from another realm, look on and applaud the actions of wicked men. Men they have convinced are masters not only of their destiny but of the destinies of those they believe they have earthly power over. They are granted, like all men, a time for repentance, but most will not repent. The judgement will be just and according to the mercy they have shown others. The final judgement of their lives is of their own doing, by their own wilful actions will they themselves be condemned.'

'Joseph, tell me who you are?' Matt asked sharply.

'Venter is coming and seeks your blood; you will see me no more,' Joseph vanished from sight.

'Davis, you pommie bastard!' Venter came bounding over the open ground towards him and before he could say anything punched him squarely in the face, his fist so large that it covered most of his face. Matt's nose exploded under the pressure and he began to lose consciousness. He felt another blow at the side of his head and a thud as he hit the ground.

Chapter 17

'Davis, Davis,' Symington's voice was whirling in Matt's head. 'Wake up.'

' Ye . . . Yes . . . Meneer,' Matt came slowly out of his stupor. 'Where am I?'

'You are in my medical centre and you are costing me money. What were you doing in the compound with the kaffirs. Don't you remember what I told you about them? It could have cost you your life.'

'It was not the kaffirs; it was that white kaffir Venter who attacked me.'

'You do not have to worry about Venter anymore. He has gone completely out of control and I am going to pay him his dues and he is going to go away with that slut of a wife of yours. Then you and I are going to share the spoils.'

'Are you sure of that?' Matt asked hopefully.

'If he does not disappear quickly I am going to have him arrested for killing your team leader Joseph, who was the only and, I can hardly bear to say it myself, the only half-decent kaffir I have ever met.'

Matt sat bolt upright, his body racked with pain, 'Joseph is dead?'

The sound of crushing silk filled his ears once more.

'Yes I assume so. Whilst you were in here for two days, someone had to do your blasting and yesterday Venter went down to your working place to blast the rounds with Joseph and only Venter came back. He was like a man traumatised as he came out of the mine. Maybe that was one kaffir too many even for Venter. He spoke to no one, got into his truck and no one has seen him since.'

'Joseph dead? I don't believe it, he is the only friend I had here, he has been closer than a brother to me.'

'Yes, yes. Whatever. Another kaffir is dead.' Symington went on without compassion, 'We have work to do and by Berriman's calculations we are only five metres from hitting the gold bar. He has changed his attitude since the latest assay surveys came in, rubbing his hands together thinking he is going to get a share of anything. The only thing he is going to get a share in is the retrenchments that I am going to announce when we have our money in the bank. You do remember what I promised you, don't you Matt?'

Matt was still in shock at the news of his friend's death. His head pulsated, his nose felt well and truly broken and, although it had been reset while he was unconscious, it looked like a small peach. He blew blood clot after blood clot into a tissue a sympathetic Symington had handed to him.

'Matt, you and I can do something now that will not only make us both rich but means we can put all this behind us. With the kind of money we will have, there is nothing we cannot buy or do. Do not let this misguided love of a dead kaffir detract you from a greater purpose. We are almost there. I can taste it.'

Matt blew hard into the tissue, 'You're an evil racist bastard with not one shred of decency in your entire body.'

'I will take that as a compliment, I have worked hard at it over the years. Now stop this childish point scoring and let us get to work. Can you start back in the morning?'

'Tomorrow's Sunday isn't it?'

'Yes, and so what?'

'Well, we aren't allowed to blast on a Sunday are we?'

'That never stopped you before did it, when I promised you extra bonus?'

'True, but there is something I need to do tomorrow.'

'Something more important than hitting the gold bar and making yourself very rich? I just don't get it; you pommies are a dumb limey lot.'

'Listen,' said Matt sharply, 'I will do what I need to do tomorrow or you can stick your money and your gold bar where the sun doesn't shine.'

'Okay, okay Matt, calm down. What is so important?'

'I have to go to Joseph's wife and family and tell them the news. They will be expecting him home on leave at the end of month. It is only fair, and they will be devastated.'

Symington rolled his eyes in disbelief and asked, 'Do you have your car?'

'No, Sarah has taken it.'

'Well, you can buy as many and whatever kind of cars you want soon, can't you? Go to security and ask Klars to give you the keys to Meneer Coetzee's Mercedes.'

'Meneer Coetzee's Mercedes! Won't he mind?' Matt showed complete surprise at the offer.

'Not anymore he won't.' Symington gave a big grin. 'He won't be showing his face around anytime soon. He received some very bad news recently, the kind of news that brings shame on a man's name and certain death. If he was any kind of man the shame alone would've been enough for him to get a length of rope and hang himself.'

'What do you mean?'

'He has received just punishment for the error of his ways. Did he think he could keep having sex with young kaffir girls and not get that new HIV Aids? It is endemic in the black population.'

'Oh no, that's terrible. I know that he should not have been doing that with any kind of young girl but that is terrible news and terrible bad luck on him.'

'Luck had nothing to do with it,' Symington replied nonchalantly.

'You did that to him?' Matt gasped. 'How you could do that to anyone?'

'I did nothing,' Symington smiled from ear to ear. 'I was simply providing the goods and services which he ordered. He got the goods he asked for, it was just so, so unfortunate that one infected kaffir girl managed to slip through the screening process. But what that means to you and me is that we can take our spoils without that German pig interfering. He has enough to think about right now as his wife will be getting her own letter anytime soon saying that he has passed it on to her as well. What goes around comes around, I find.'

Matt was speechless for a moment.

'I take it back when I said you were evil. You are beyond evil. If there is such a thing.'

'Why thank you,' Symington revelled in the accolade. 'Now get out of that bed and go and see that kaffir friend's family so you can be back here for Monday morning. They live four hours away in Zululand.'

'I will get you your gold bar, and take my money, and then I will be taking no more orders from you, or anyone else like you, the rest of my life. And I hope that your share will rot in hell with you and your kind.'

'Touché,' replied Symington. 'Touché. Now get going.'

***

'Hello,' Matt entered the hut of Joseph's family with his eyes and head bowed low. 'I am Matt Davis. I was working with your husband Joseph for the last ten months and we became good friends, which is why I come to bring you some very sad news.'

Joseph's wife Martha hugged her three youngest children close to her as Matt said what he had come to say. He finished with, 'I am very, very sorry. He was a good, honest man and I loved him.'

Martha wailed and screamed, 'No, no, no. It cannot be, it cannot be.'

Matt went over to try and console her but was held back by a large black man who had appeared from another room and who indicated to Matt that they should go outside.

Once outside he said in broken English, 'Plees. Come me.'

He led Matt to a clearing on the edge of town where there were both stone grave markers and wooden ones with Zulu markings, since brothers were laid together whether Christian or not. The man pointed towards the centre of the graveyard and said, 'For chiefs.'

Matt walked over to a large gravestone that drew his eye and what he saw made him stagger back. It read: Into the hands of God Joseph Tetu son of Tetu Umlayne a Zulu Chief and tribal leader of the Province of Eshetu born 8th January 1943 died 16th July 1983.

Three years earlier! Matt could not take it in. Was this some sort of sick joke? No, worse, a nightmare from which he could not wake up?

He got into the car and drove back. A torrent of questions in his mind. The harder he thought the less sense everything made.

If Joseph had died three years before he arrived, then who was the Joseph he'd befriended and been working with? It made no sense. The sound of crushing silk filled his ears. Each time he heard it, it became louder, like a noise magnified by a confined place.

Matt found it very difficult to sleep that night even though the sound of Sarah's constant complaining had ceased. The house was eerily quiet. He'd had no more experiences of the unknown since the evening of the spiritual battle and the subsequent blessing. He was no longer concerned about the house since his life was now at an unforeseen crossroads.

He started to go over his experiences since he'd first arrived in Africa and tried to find something that tied the threads together, but couldn't. His eyes were heavier than they had ever been. He felt emotionally and physically drained, more than empty. He began to question the sound of crushing silk he'd heard in his times of trial, almost a pointer of things to come. He started to feel afraid but then remembered, irrespective of how difficult the situations had been, the sound had been strangely comforting and had brought him some element of peace. Finally succumbing to exhaustion he fell asleep at two thirty to a voice in his head saying, 'Never be afraid if I am not there. If I am not there I have no need to be, but when I am, it is time.' Soothing, comforting words that Matt took to heart, believing it to be his long-dead mother whose loving presence had never fully left him.

Chapter 18

'Temba, are you my new team leader?'

The rough-looking Basotho standing in front of Matt nodded. The Basotho were the fiercest of all the African tribes and appeared devoid of any emotion, especially when taking another man's life. He was one of Symington's Boys' Brigade with a reputation as a warrior who always took a trophy from those he killed.

The trophy would be whatever took his fancy in the moments after the kill: one eyebrow or both; the top lip of a Zulu, since they protruded more than most; the tip of the penis. But for all his ostentatious masculine warrior traits he had a thirst for what the Bible calls 'the strange flesh' of another man. Not that many of his homosexual conquests lived to tell the tale. But Temba lacked the intelligence for a team leader, he was there as Symington's eyes and ears, and Matt knew it.

'How many machines do we have drilling?'

'Eight,' replied Temba.

'Eight? In a cross cut?' Matt was surprised.

'Yes. Baas Symington wants two blasts today and two on the night shift.'

'Since when do we blast on the night shift?'

'Since now,' Temba replied, looking fixedly at Matt.

This man was showing no kind of respect at all, he was doing Symington's bidding and Matt started to feel a bit surplus to requirements and in real danger. He wondered why Symington was including him. His Boys' Brigade were more than capable of doing the blasting. The law stated they couldn't, but the law had never stopped Symington doing anything he wanted to do. Matt was alarmed at the sound of the machines in the tunnels. Even if there were eight of them drilling the noise from a hundred metres away was deafening. He went to investigate.

As he entered the cross cut tunnel entrance he heard high pressure jackhammers working at two thousand psi, but there was no water spray or vapour coming from any of the machines. He realised that none of them were actually drilling. The operators had turned off their machines because the noise was deafening, but the noise level didn't alter. They were holding their ears against a sound that was becoming painful. Two of the operators threw down their machines and ran out of the tunnel shouting, 'Ion dow yena mooby kanjani', meaning 'there is great evil in this place'.

Matt stood with his hands over his ears and felt the sound drumming against his hands. He could see that Temba was very afraid, his eyes protruded, his mouth was slightly open, gasping in air that was now thick with machine fog and water vapour. But the machines were still switched off.

The ventilation pipes that circulated the air at the face by pulling fresh air from the main tunnels into the cross cuts started to vibrate, as though a mighty hand was battering them. The pipes, which were a metre across and made of steel sheeting, started to buckle in places just like a crushed beer can. Matt could not believe what he was looking at and for a moment allowed himself to feel that he was having another nightmare. Then a final blow on the end of pipe closed it up like it was made of tin foil and everyone ran out of the tunnel.

Temba looked back and Matt turned with him, 'Temba, are you afraid?'

Temba looked menacing, 'I fear nothing of this earth but this is not of this earth. It is only the fact that I would suffer horribly in the white man's prison, that I don't slit your throat where you stand for what you have done. But I will have my moment and my moment will be your last.'

He disappeared. Matt had heard some pretty stark personal threats during his time in the mine and he had just put two fingers up, physically and emotionally, but that threat was so chilling and said with such callousness that he trembled violently and was almost physically sick.

He turned to look at a machine operator who had just come out of the cross cuts, his eyes had turned blood red and he was frothing at the mouth, then he was thrown to the ground like a rag by an immense power. The young man began writhing and spitting like a snake, his body contorted beyond human capability, then he suddenly straightened out like a board and died as a formless black apparition left his gaping mouth.

'I am not working with that Basotho dog for a moment more!' Matt shouted as he walked into Symington's office.

Symington lifted his head from the mine plan covering his desk, the red area now showed a cross cut almost intersecting it.

'Are we through?' demanded Symington. 'Are we through? Did you hit it?' he almost screamed.

Temba was also in the room, sitting on the floor to the left of the door. He kept his head down but Matt could see that he had taken a beating. His eyes and head were bruised and the dried red mash at his hairline showed that he had been bleeding from a wound caused by Symington's cane.

Matt had always objected to Symington's over-indulgence in doling out discipline with his cane but he wondered if the beating resulted from reports of Temba's threat to Matt.

'That serves you right that does,' Matt said in Temba's direction.

'What serves what right?' Symington was confused.

'That team leader of yours threatening to kill me, of course. You did beat him for that?'

'You did what, kaffir?'

Symington turned towards Temba, exploded into a rage and bounded across the office with his cane in his hand, lifting it high to strike Temba again who covered his head and begged, 'No Baas. No more please.'

Symington held the cane above Temba's lowered head and said, 'If you ever threaten one of my chosen men again I will kill you myself.'

Chosen men, thought Matt, well that was a turnaround. He thought of Venter, who had not been seen for weeks, neither had Sarah. The rumour was that they were holed up in the mine flats awaiting the birth of their adulterous offspring. Matt had come to understand that Symington hated the Afrikaner shift bosses more than he hated the pommies. He just played whichever side gave him the most advantage; and probably had neither trust nor faith in either.

He turned back towards Matt, 'Are you okay? He won't trouble you again and although he is a Basotho dog I want him there with you underground when we break through. Send him immediately to me when you break through and I will come underground and help you get the gold out.' He lowered his voice, it was both questioning and desperate, 'Are we through Matt?'

'No. Did that dog not tell you that we have some evil and strange things going on and everyone is spooked by them. I have just watched one of machine operators become possessed by something and then it took his life.'

'Which machine operator?' asked Biltong, who had just walked into the office. 'You only have eight and I have just collected eight from the station.'

'No, you can't have, you're mistaken. I watched one of them die I'm telling you. The machines were making a noise but weren't drilling and then the vent pipe began to crush like a tin foil and we just ran out of the tunnel . . .' Matt stopped in mid-speech as the man he had watched die not more than twenty minutes before stood in the doorway. 'Temba tell them. Tell them Temba. You were there.'

'I know nothing of what you say,' he replied without lifting his head, 'and I never threatened to kill you. This gold you seek is making you mad. You have the gold fever and it is making you crazy with greed.'

'Shut it kaffir,' barked Symington. 'I have heard enough. Matt, go home. Get some rest and be back at four in the morning. Let us finish this job.'

Matt was not really listening. He was traumatised by the events he absolutely believed he had recently witnessed.

He drove home, still in Coetzee's Mercedes. Africa had changed him more than he could understand. Had he become a bad man? Had he been a bad man before he came? Or was he just waking up to the fact that he was exactly what his father had called him during their only meeting when he was twenty-seven, 'You're a bastard child and you will always be a bastard child. Fatherless you came into this world and fatherless you will leave it.' Matt's mother however, throughout her life, had fiercely denied that accusation.

But now Matt felt that he was just what Temba had said, another white man sickened by greed, he could not deny it. He had come to Africa for money and no other reason and he knew that was a real truth. Yet now, with what should have been the answer to all his hopes and dreams lying twenty-four hours ahead of him, there was neither excitement nor exhilaration at the thought. He would only be a richer bastard child than he'd been before. He sobbed openly as he sat in the car outside the house.

To be rich and not have the love he so desperately needed was like dipping a pig into gold paint. It was still a pig and any value was merely superficial and insubstantial, of that he was now convinced. The sound of crushing silk filled his ears when he finally lay down on his bed and fell asleep immediately.

Chapter 19

'Shoot that kaffir!' shouted Klars, the head of security, as Matt pulled into the mine car park. Bodies were lying around, some obviously dead from shotgun and bullet wounds.

'What the hell's going on?' Matt shouted at Klars.

'Hell is good choice of words. We have a riot. This Shona tribe are going mental, saying that we have mined into their heritage and spiritual ancestry, or some shit. But don't worry, I have my boys here and once we have killed enough of them they will back off.'

'Matt, Matt!' shouted Symington. 'Get over here quick.'

Matt ran across the yard with bullets whizzing around his head as mine security turned their guns on anything that moved.

'Klars, how long before we can go underground?'

'Not too long Meneer. We are up to about forty dead and they are starting to lose the spirit to fight now,' he replied, while shooting a young lad in the back who was cowering against the perimeter fence.

'It is like a bush pig shoot,' laughed one of the security guards, standing on the roof of his Land Rover and firing indiscriminately at anything that crossed his sights.

Matt was sickened to his stomach and shook his head, wondering why he was there and feeling that it was no place for him, no place for any man.

'Straighten your face and be a man. They are only kaffirs,' Symington barked at Matt. 'We have almost holed into the gold bar. This day will go down in history as one when we took back what was truly ours.'

'What was ours?' Matt snapped back. 'Nothing of this is ours. We are no more than thieves and robbers, raping and pillaging the inheritance of the blacks who, through no fault of their own, have yet to develop the skills and put the infrastructure . . .'

'Stop with that pommie sentimental, bullshit principles,' Symington said angrily. 'The only thing that principles cost you is money. Now get down the mine and get that last round blasted. When you have holed send Temba back to me and I will send a team to get that gold out. Your cheque will be waiting for you when you come out. Then you can get your sickening, kaffir-loving, limey-arsed presence out of my sight.'

Matt looked Symington straight in the eye and replied, 'It's been a pleasure doing business with you.'

Symington fumed. Matt left the office, not noticing the chaos all around him. The whole situation seemed surreal. He wondered if this was what it felt like when you were about to die. The sound of crushing silk was now often in his ears. He walked obliviously, in a dreamlike state, across the yard towards to the shaft.

Biltong was hiding in his cabin and Matt beckoned him out just as Klars said, 'Okay boys. That is enough,' and the gunfire ceased.

'I have never seen a day like this,' Biltong's hands and body were shaking. 'I just want to get out of here.'

He lifted the latch to open the shaft gate and a group of young black men jeered as he did so. They fell silent when the guns of Klars's men turned towards them.

'I don't suppose you really want to know,' Biltong whispered, 'but Venter is dead. He was on the way to hospital to see the birth of his child this morning. The police phoned here asking who the next of kin was.'

'So, how did he die?'

'Well, it seems like he was on the way to the hospital, like I said, and he was taking home his latest conquest on the way, no surprise there then, when his lady friend decided she wanted a bit more of him on the way. She obviously bit off more than she could chew, so to speak, and they ploughed into a road bridge killing them both instantly. I did say he would get his one day.'

Biltong smiled and replaced the latch on the gate with Matt inside the cage ready to go down. Biltong gave the man riding signal of three rings and the cage started to move downwards.

'Seems like history repeats itself. As one bastard child leaves this world another one enters it,' Biltong's voice disappeared as the cage dropped.

'What do you mean?' Matt shouted as the cage descended.

***

'Koos , Koos!' wailed Sarah as their baby made its appearance into the world. This was not the dream ending she had hoped for. Cradling the child to her breast she would not be pacified by the policewoman who had broken the news. There had been no mention of the presence of his passenger and the compromising situation that they had been found in; the officer in her sympathy had spared Sarah that indignity.

***

'Temba!' Symington called him into his office.

'Yes Baas?'

'It is time to complete our plan. Go underground and watch for when the tunnel holes. Keep the entry small, only one metre by one metre.'

'Why this size, Baas?'

'Think about it. Once the tunnel is holed and that bastard Englishman climbs into that small place, you can take your moment as he has no way of escape.'

Temba smiled and nodded.

'Then make sure the entire gold bar is transported to the shaft by the end of shift and when you come to surface your money will be waiting for you.'

Symington walked with Temba across the yard towards where Biltong had the cage waiting with the rest of the squad of Symington's Boys' Brigade. As soon as the cage had gone below surface level Symington turned to Biltong and gave his orders.

'That is the last time I want to see those kaffir's faces. As soon as the last skip of gold bar has been hoisted, throw the power switch to the shaft and leave them down there.'

'What? Without food or water, Meneer?' Biltong asked.

'Yes, let them feed on each other like the cockroaches they are.'

Biltong looked at Symington, 'Your father, my uncle, would be so proud of you. What a master plan you have worked to get back the family fortune.'

They hugged like brothers.

***

'Temba, there you are. There is only half a round drilled, it will only break about a metre or so. Let's drill some more holes and get this finished,' Matt said as Temba and the rest of the Boys' Brigade entered the cross cut.

Temba took hold of Matt's wrist as he went to pick up a tin of spray paint to mark off the holes for drilling.

'No. Meneer Symington said only a hole a metre wide.'

'Let go of my hand,' Matt looked directly at Temba, 'and remember what Meneer Symington said about you making any threats or gestures to me.'

The Boys' Brigade laughed out loud, to a man. Temba turned to his team and they stopped laughing immediately as he drew his knife from his belt. Matt tried to loosen Temba's grip on his wrist as fear swept over him. Temba moved his body towards Matt's with the knife at waist height. Matt breathed a deep sigh of relief as Temba went past him to a box of explosives sitting unopened on the ground and slit the lid open, exposing the cartridges.

Chapter 20

'Hold them back!' shouted Klars as the armed security guards were overpowered by hundreds of Shona who appeared from nowhere. They had killed many and the bodies of Shona brothers lay all around, stacked onto pickup trucks ready to be taken to the morgue.

This sight only fuelled the anger of these most formidable of warriors. The security guards now begged for mercy as their weapons were taken from them, but were bludgeoned with their own guns and any other weapons the tribesmen had to hand. Symington, panic-stricken, had bolted the office door and taken out his revolver from its drawer. He was thinking of exiting the mine complex via the back gate in the opposite direction. Concluding that once it had quietened down he would come back later with Biltong and hoist the load of lucre.

As Symington cowered in his office some Shona battered on the door. He quickly opened the back door to make his escape. The frame of his, supposedly, recently-dead pikanin, Sela stood before him with a machete in his hand.

'But you are dead, I saw your burned body, I read the suicide note.'

Symington, now in a state of sheer terror, retreated back into the office and tried to lock the door. But it was too late. Sela was behind him with five of his warrior brothers and they were going to exact vengeance of the worst possible kind and Symington knew it. He shook so violently that the gun he was holding fell from his hand. He wept like a child, fell to his knees and held out his cane in an attempt to placate Sela, whom he had forgotten was of the Shona tribe. He offered him the instrument of correction with pleas for mercy, hoping that Sela would simply beat him in like manner and praying that that would be the end of it. Symington began feverishly trying to work out a plan to save himself.

Sela said nothing and just nodded towards Symington's locked safe. Symington did not care about the few thousand rand that was in there, he just wanted to escape.

'Take it, take it,' he smiled at Sela and handed him the key with a trembling hand. Sela nodded to a young warrior to take the keys and open the safe.

'I am so glad you are alive,' Symington began, grinning madly. 'I have great news. That German pig of a mine manager who raped your sister has been infected with AIDS. I made sure he was not going to get away with it.'

Sela still made no gesture and said no words. He just looked intently at Symington who had laid the cane at his feet.

'And Venter, that evil devil, has died only this morning along with some whore. And that pommie is on his last shift as Temba is going to finish him today for trying to take your gold bar. No! No! Sorry your spiritual heritage. That is right is it not it, Sela my friend?' Symington continued pathetically.

The office was silent. You could hear a pin drop. Outside, however, the cries of men being tortured could be heard as the white guards not quite bludgeoned to death were now undergoing the worst kind of passage out of this life by being necklaced.

Sela nodded at the mine plan still lying open on the table, the red area was dotted in black ink showing calculations in US dollars of the value the hoard of gold would gross.

'I will share it with you,' Symington whimpered. 'You and the boys here. We can all be rich Sela!'

'We are not, and never have been, your boys. We are men from the Shona tribe. Your guns and laws no longer have any power over us. You are now our boys.' His voice had a presence much greater than the stature of the man. He then picked up the cane from the floor and began circling Symington.

'We are going to beat you, like you beat us. We are going to rape your young girls, like you raped ours. We are going to take your wealth, the way you took it from us. And then we are going to kill you like dogs, the way you killed our people during your apartheid. That era now ends and a new South Africa begins on this day.'

'That wasn't me!' protested Symington. 'That was the Afrikaner. I am a Rhodesian. We loved the black man, we fed the whole of Africa, my father . . .' he carried on as he was helped from the floor by four warriors and brought to the table. '. . . was a wealthy landowner who brought prosperity to the black in Rhodesia.'

Sela looked intently at him, 'Your father was no better than you. He too, was a just a white kaffir. It seems to me that it makes no difference what the colour of a man's skin is. If he is blinded by greed, with an intense desire to have more at any cost; if he believes he is superior in all ways to other men; if he has let fear or the need for vengeance control his soul and then, through that fear or need for vengeance, tries to force the will of another; then that man has become nothing more than a mere kaffir!'

'You surprise me Sela. You are obviously a man of learning. I sadly underestimated you,' Symington said sheepishly. 'I should have made you a team leader.'

Sela smiled, 'I am the son of a chief. Your offers mean nothing. They cannot add anything that I don't already have, that is truly important. It is not as you think that the black man does not have the capacity to learn and that he is just an ignorant kaffir, a hewer of wood and a carrier of water at the white man's bidding. How can any man study and better himself in life with a jackboot on his neck? Sadly for you that knowledge is only in my head. The years of oppression and hatred have prevented it from moving to my heart and making me the man that all true men should be. I am at this moment still as you have said many times before, just a kaffir.'

He then took hold of Symington's head and pushed it down onto the plan so he could see the marked out red area. The warriors held him firmly so that he could not resist, although Symington showed little resistance, his whole body had gone into shock. He wept like a juvenile about to be beaten for misbehaviour.

Sela broke the cane in half over his knee. He placed the spiked end against Symington's temple, then thumped it through the man's head with the butt of Symington's own gun until it was driven through to the table top and held his fat, sagging body in place.

***

'That's it,' said Matt, 'the last of the explosives are in the holes. Let's retreat to the safe side and blast this lot out. It looks like pay day.'

He patted Temba in a friendly way on the shoulder. Temba made no response. The fifteen shots were fired but the concussion was much louder than expected. So much so, that the miners fell to the ground from the force of air.

'Bloody hell!' Matt exclaimed picking himself up. 'That was crazy.'

He looked at Temba who made no response. As they walked back to the blasting area Matt was already planning his escape. He would go to the blast site and, if it had holed, he would quickly inspect it, take a small nugget as a sample to show Symington, and then send the boys in before making a quick exit to surface while they were washing everything down. 'Wait here. I will go and check if all the holes have blasted.'

As he walked into the cross cut he felt uneasy and looked over his shoulder, wary about being followed. At the blast site he stooped down to clamber over the broken rock and shone his cap light inside the small cavern. The light shone back, refracted into many smaller beams.

Matt had never seen anything like it. As the smoke cleared he could see a vein of gold. It looked almost pure, at least two thousand grams per ton he thought. There was buckshot gold hanging all around, like clusters of grapes. So this is what happens when the Black Reef and Carbon Leader meet, he thought.

He went back up the tunnel for fifty yards to get a water hose. He could not contain his excitement any longer, even the sounds of crushing silk now filling his ears did little to dampen it. He feverishly dragged the hose to the hole and started to wash the cavern down. The more water that went in, the brighter the reflection. Matt was almost euphoric and, gripped by gold-fevered adrenaline, paid little heed to the lights of the Boys' Brigade coming down the tunnel towards him.

Eventually he started giving instructions to get the picks and hessian sacks and said, 'We are rich boys. We are rich!'

'Are you sure it is not fool's gold?' asked Temba.

'Fool's gold? I have seen that and I have been mining fool's gold all my life in one way or another. No! This is the real stuff. Come and see, come and see,' he beckoned Temba to join him as he turned to re-enter the cavern.

Temba followed, drawing his knife from his belt. Matt bent down and picked up a solid gold nugget of some three ounces. He thought, this would make some beautiful wedding rings for a happy couple and slipped it into his breast pocket. Matt had been many things in his life but never a thief and reflected that when all those around you are lawless and wicked (thinking particularly of Symington and Venter) something rubs off and that he was therefore innocent in the matter.

Matt turned back towards the entrance where Temba was just starting to come through. There was a loud bang, the ground shook violently; a second loud bang brought a huge area of stone down into the cavern as the fault planes shifted, crushing Temba and completely sealing off the cavern from the tunnel.

Matt lay semi-conscious on the ground. His helmet had fallen forward and a large rock had struck him on the back of his head. The super-heated blood that races through a body when working in deep mining now started to run down his face and into his mouth. He spat the blood out and attempted to stand up. The sound of his racing heart pounded in his ears. He couldn't get up. His heart began to slow as his lifeblood drained away.

The events of the last year of his life now started to play out in his mind. What a fool he had been. He now lay dying for fool's gold. He concluded in his final moments that even real gold is fool's gold when it costs men's lives to get it. That thought beat in his mind for several moments, his heart broke, he wept. He had just strength enough to reach into his breast pocket and remove the nugget. He brought his hand towards his face so that he could see it, now covered with blood and displaying the true price of gold. Matt raised his hand and the gold lit up the darkness all around.

The sound of crushing silk filled his ears, so close he could almost touch it. In agony he stared across the cavern through the mingled sweat, blood and tears to where the noise was coming from. A lone figure stood gazing at him.

'Joseph? Joseph, is that you?' he spluttered through the blood filling his mouth.

As the sound filled the cavern along with a golden light wings six feet across unfurled before his eyes, making a sound of crushing silk and the figure spoke, 'Into the hands of God.'

Chapter 21

Matt's body was found some twelve months later by workers for the new mine owners, a consortium of black African investors. They had taken over the gold mining industry by buying up the mining rights of West Rand Consolidated Mines for a fraction of their market value. Matt had, by all accounts, ignited a flame that had set the whole forest ablaze, as Joseph had predicted.

The rioting that had initially started because of the theft of the Shona's inheritance spread like wildfire throughout the gold mining industry. The unions seized the opportunity to fight for improved pay and conditions and the industry, like the apartheid regime that ran it, crumbled. The gold lay untouched for almost a year while government and local elections took place.

But what had really changed? The new rulers of the country simply engaged in their own form of apartheid, little different to the previous. The only change being the colour of the man holding the power. Under the new system of apartheid, called affirmative action and known elsewhere as positive discrimination, no white person was to be given a job that a black person could do, irrespective of their level of qualification.

The only piece of gold found in the cavern by the team that uncovered Matt's body was the nugget in Matt's decayed hand. All the surrounding rock was just typical quartzite. Matt's nugget was processed and made into two wedding bands.

Matt's real contribution to the ending of apartheid would never be known. He would not receive the Nobel Peace Prize like others involved in the ending of apartheid movement. Matt believed that he would find a true reason and purpose to his life in wealth and material gain but he lost his life in the process. Some might say that he actually found life by making his peace with God and gaining an afterlife.

How many, like Matt, have their eyes on a goal that they will probably never reach, using each and every day to prepare for a greater tomorrow, which sadly for many never comes? How many times do we see those about to take hold of what they have struggled simply die and leave it to those who have not earned it? In many cases they have lost family, friends, marriages and even their own souls believing that wealth alone was a real reason and purpose for life. As the Psalmist says: 'all is vanity and a chasing after the wind.'

We spend our lifetimes chasing the things of time instead of the things of eternity, an eternity that is in the heart of every person, should they choose to look for it. Indeed, what did the many men who lost their lives in opposing the white apartheid regime really achieve when one version of apartheid was simply replaced by another?

Sela's words will forever be true the world over, no matter what race or colour holds power, because a change of regime or political policy can never deal with the real problem that faces humankind, a problem solely of the heart:

It seems to me that it makes no difference what the colour of a man's skin is. If he is blinded by greed, with an intense desire to have more at any cost; if he believes he is superior in all ways to other men; if he has let fear or the need for vengeance control his soul and then, through that fear or need for vengeance, tries to force the will of another; then that man has become nothing more than a mere kaffir!

It is a problem which each one of us must deal with alone because racism has nothing to do with the colour of a person's skin, it is only ever to do with the heart of the one who can see no deeper than skin itself. The simple truth is that all men are born equal and their lives have equal value to our own.

About the author

Keith Brown has been presenting to businesses for almost 20 years, having left the mining industry in the early 1990s. His career continued within the IT industry in several marketing and sales positions. Since 2010 Keith has worked as a conference speaker and civil celebrant. He is married to his second wife, Viktoriya, and lives in Nottinghamshire.

His own story involves him being caught up in an explosion underground, recorded at the time as a mining accident although it was attempted murder. It resulted in him losing 20% of his lungs and hearing but merely galvanised his determination not to be beaten by the apartheid regime. He went on to become, at 27, the youngest man in South Africa to ever run a gold mine as a Mine Captain – managing a budget of $5m a month and 350 multicultural employees.

He still bears the physical disability from that near fatal encounter, but holds the mindset that the experience over 2,000 meters below surface positively changed his life and business values forever:

If we are still alive we have opportunity and, for the brave, an opportunity is all that is needed.

www.keithbrownspeaking.com